TERRA ELECTRICA:
THE GUARDIANS OF
THE NORTH

TERRA ELECTRICA: THE GUARDIANS OF THE NORTH

Antonia Maxwell

NEEM TREE
PRESS

Published by Neem Tree Press Limited 2024
Copyright © Antonia Maxwell, 2024
Antonia Maxwell asserts her rights under the Copyright, Designs and Patents Act 1988 to be recognized as the author of this work.

1 3 5 7 9 10 8 6 4 2

Neem Tree Press Limited
95A Ridgmount Gardens, London, WC1E 7AZ
info@neemtreepress.com
www.neemtreepress.com

A catalogue record for this book is available from the British Library.

ISBN 978-1-915584-11-3 Paperback
ISBN 978-1-915584-12-0 UK Ebook
ISBN 978-1-915584-70-0 US Ebook

Printed and bound in Great Britain

For Maia, Finn, and Theo

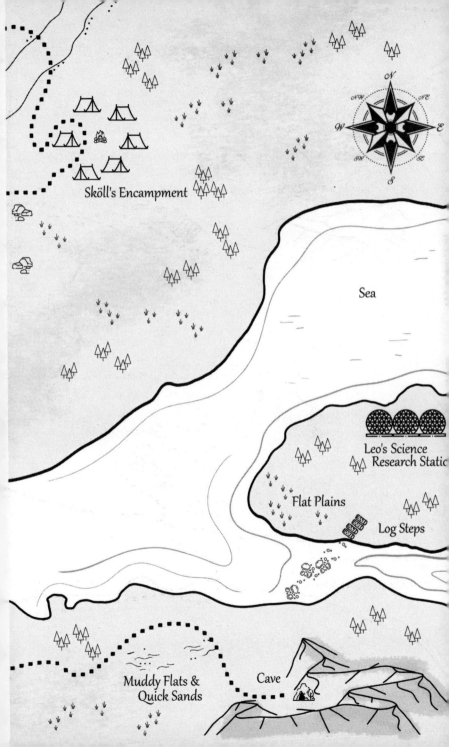

Sköll's Encampment

Sea

Leo's Science
Research Station

Flat Plains

Log Steps

Muddy Flats &
Quick Sands

Cave

Chapter 1

O *uch.* It hurt. When Mani tried to pinch the flame, the way her father did, it was hot, and stung. Her father could extinguish the candle with his big flat thumb and finger in a single resolute *pffffssst*. But, when Mani tried it, the flame flickered around her fingers and wouldn't go out.

Today Mani wished more than ever that her father would return.

She blew the candle out as usual, and even that took a few puffs. She was getting weaker from hunger each day. But out it must go—too much had burned down already. She wouldn't light it again till tomorrow. A thumb-width of candlelight a day—that was all she was allowed.

Her father had set out the rules before he left. There were always rules. Each time, before Mani lit the candle, she marked a thumb-width first by pressing a nick into the wax with her fingernail. When it burned down to the mark—out it went. That was it—because they had to make it last if they were to survive. Mani never disobeyed her father.

She watched the curl of grey smoke rise through the darkness to the top of the cave and inhaled the peppery charcoal smell. Perhaps she didn't need the candlelight today anyway. The moon outside was high and bright and illuminated the craggy walls of the cave. In any case, the orange flame threw flickering shadows against the wall, and made dark forms that Mani half recognized from her dreams. And they worried her. So, in some ways, it was better with it out.

The moon, her mother would have said. *The moon will show you the way.* And that thought right now made her feel less alone.

But it couldn't take away the hunger. Because one thing Mani knew more than anything else—she had never *ever* felt hunger like this before. It was like her growling, howling stomach had moved to her head and was giving her wild crazy dreams of breaking free from the safety of the cave and going to find food.

Ever since her father had left, Mani had been living alone in the cave. The polar night had descended, and the sun had dipped below the horizon where it would stay for a whole month. Mani had got used to the dark, although she didn't like to think about it too much. There were some things that helped—and now, in the blackness, came the soft slow beat of enormous wings, followed by a gentle yip and wheeze.

Yip-yip-wee-oooh, yip-yip-wee-oooh.

The short-eared owl came to rest on the ledge at the entrance to the cave. It arrived at the same time every day. And at the same time every day, Mani took one of the small pieces of chalkstone her father had given her and dragged it down the wall (just as her father had shown her) next to the other marks. The sun might have disappeared, but the owl's routine never changed. Mani counted the marks again. Twenty-nine. This was how many days her father had been gone. He'd said it would take four days to reach fresh ground, and he would return straight away. He'd promised. But he still hadn't come back. And Mani *must not leave the cave*. This is what he'd said. He hadn't given a reason why. He never gave reasons. But Mani knew better than to question him. Nobody ever challenged her father. Everybody listened to him, bowing—flinching—under his leadership that had kept the village safe for all those years.

Each day, Mani sat waiting obediently for him to return. But how much longer could she wait? The hunger hurt, like a wild cat was inside her stomach, punching and clawing.

Before he left, her father had also told her that, when the owl came to the cave, as it did every day, it was time to eat. *Do not forget to eat and drink.* And so, as if her father was there giving her the command, Mani now crawled to the back wall of the cave, feeling her way along the rough ground, and picked up the last jar of *rak-rak* they had stored there. Pickled rat—it was all they had. She sat

3

on the soft sealskin in the centre of the cave and, in the darkness, stuffed the sour chunks into her mouth. She was hungry and didn't care what it tasted like anymore. In any case, there wasn't anything else to eat.

That would change when her father returned. He'd promised. Mani wondered what he would bring. Probably fresh seal—he always brought seal, even though it was rare now—and sweet berries. And perhaps he would have been to the trading post and exchanged precious seal oil and skin for biscuits and chocolate. And maybe he would have caught fresh fish—pink salmon and tender shellfish. Mani closed her eyes and imagined she was eating mouthfuls of the warm fish soup that her mother used to make. She swallowed the thought with a gulp, along with the half-chewed pickled rat, and wiped her eyes.

For now, she had no choice but to keep on waiting.

Chapter 2

Mani's mother was dead. She had died with the others. They were all gone—the whole village. The disease—if that's what it was—had spared no one except for her and her father. But Mani had never said goodbye to her.

They had to leave—she and her father—because they were the only ones left. There was *danger everywhere*, her father said. They had no choice. They had to get away from where the disease had hit—their village, their home—and hide while he worked out what to do. So little was known about the terrible sickness, other than that it was unlike anything the world had seen before. And it was deadly.

But it had all happened so quickly. Mani could hardly believe Matka had gone. In the end, her father had not let Mani see her. The disease was merciless and grotesque. Mani had wanted to cry, but she had dug her fingernails into the palms of her hands to quell the tears. Her father had been angry—angry with the *zientzia*, the science-men who had brought this to them. *Always meddling. They could never leave things alone.* They thought they knew it all, but their wisdom was shallow.

It had all happened too fast; her mother's voice still rang in her head, and her smell still lingered on her clothes. It was really like she might appear at any moment. And this was what Mani wanted most in all the world.

Mani had watched her father pack. He had piled all he could onto the old dog sled. He'd asked Mani if there was anything else she wanted to bring—*but she had to be quick.* What should she bring? The thing she treasured most in all the world—the knife with the whalebone handle that her father had given her on her twelfth birthday—was easy. It came with a belted leather holster, and she wore it all the time.

But there had been something else. Just as they were leaving, she had seen the wooden mask hanging on the wall of her bedroom. It was oval, with elongated holes for eyes, and was painted white and decorated with feathers and flecks of turquoise paint. It had hung there for as long as Mani could remember—*and there it must stay*, her mother had always said. It was a very special mask, and one day it would be Mani's, but not until she was old enough.

"Can I bring that?" she asked her father, pointing up at the wall. They both stopped and stared at the mask.

6

Then her father reached up and took it down. He handed it to Mani, although he didn't let go for a few seconds. Mani locked eyes with her father. It was of no use to anyone here, in the lost village with all the dead people. And no use to her mother, now she was dead too.

Mani had been both pleased and surprised as her father released it, and she tucked it straight into the caribou-skin bag that she used for school.

"It's yours," he said, but his face looked uncertain, and his mouth moved as if he wanted to say more.

She hugged the bag to her chest.

Mani and her father had then left their home, dragging the loaded sled up the riverbanks as far as they could into the hills. By nightfall, they had ended up here in the cave, where they had remained ever since, working out what to do next.

Mani sat in the darkness now, holding the mask and running her fingers over the feathers. She did this every day. Just holding it made her feel closer to her old life, and to her mother.

"What's it for?" she'd asked, many, many times. She would stand and study it, hanging on the wall in her bedroom. "Can I put it on? Why is it special?"

"You'll find out," her mother would say. "In time. Don't be in a hurry. It's not a toy. It was gifted to you when you were a baby. But you've much to learn first. You must wait until you are older. You will know when. Then you can take it down and try it on. I will be here to guide you."

7

Well, she was older, wasn't she? And it wasn't a question of hurrying. There was nothing else to do here. Matka wasn't here to guide her anymore. And her father had not come home. So why shouldn't she try the mask on?

Mani stared into its expressionless wooden face. It looked white and ghostly in the moonlight. It wasn't so special anyway, was it? Just an old piece of painted wood with turquoise splatters and a few feathers stuck on? But now, inside the dark empty cave, as she held it in her hands and gazed into it, something very strange started to happen. The white-painted wood began to shimmer with pale green light. Then, as she kept watching, it glimmered turquoise and blue. The mask seemed to become weightless—almost fizzing in her hands. The turquoise feathers lit up like green-blue flames and peeled away, floating and dancing in the air around her.

Mani flung the mask from her hand and it landed on the ground at her feet with a clatter. As it fell, the lights extinguished. Once again, it was just a circular piece of wood with holes for eyes, decorated with feathers, and an old leather strap attached to either side. She stared down at it. What was happening? Had she imagined it? Was the hunger making her see things?

She reached forward and picked the mask up again. She would put it away. She needed to keep her mind clear and be strong for her father when he finally returned. But something stopped her. She didn't want to put it away. She held it in her lap. Something about it drew her in and, as her focus settled on it again, the same thing happened. The mask started to glow and shimmer, and blue-green lights bubbled out from it and filled the air around her. She sat still and watched. It was quite beautiful—the cave was filled with glittering lights and her hands and arms were covered in veils of turquoise and green. Without thinking, she raised the mask above her head and pulled it down over her face, hooking the strap behind her head and over her ears.

At first, she could only feel the fizzing surface of the mask against her cheeks; the eyeholes were too high up and she couldn't see through them. She shut her eyes. She took a deep, deep breath.

The rush of air through her body made her dizzy, like she was falling, and she felt sick. Perhaps it was the hunger, but the only thing she could do to stop the feeling was to open her eyes. When she opened them, she found she was no longer in the dark cave, and she wasn't looking out from behind the mask. She was standing on snow. And around her were endless vistas of pure white. And there was light, bleaching white light. And, above, blue skies and yellow sunshine. All around, there were glistening hills and valleys of ice and snow as far as she could see.

"Hello?" she called out, spinning around on the snow. *Could this be real?* she thought. "Is there anybody here?"

Somehow, she had a strong feeling that her mother was near. But that couldn't be true. Her mother was dead. And she couldn't see anyone. But she called out anyway.

"Mother? Matka? Are you here?"

She started walking up the slope in front of her. Perhaps, at the top, she would get a better view? The snow squeaked underfoot, and the air was thin and cold and made her pant for breath. When she reached the top, she stopped and looked around, blinking in the sunshine and snow glare.

Suddenly, she felt a push from behind, in the centre of her back, and something big and soft caused her to lose her balance. She was tumbling back over the powdery snow to where she had started. As she rolled and slid down the slope, she became aware of the sound of heavy running and a noisy snorting beside her, and through the spray of snow she could see big white padded paws and a huge white furry body thundering along next to her. Eventually, they reached the bottom of the slope and came to a stop. Mani was lying on her back. She sat up.

She was looking into two deep black eyes and a big black wet nose set in a white furry face. It was a polar bear. Mani recognized it from some of the old photographs she'd seen, although bears had long been extinct. The bear seemed to be looking back at her in a kindly but inquisitive way.

The bear moved towards Mani and sniffed the air around her head. Then it extended a huge paw, held it near Mani's chin and inspected her face. Mani could feel the bear's warm breath on her cheeks.

"You're supposed to be older," the bear muttered, "but it's definitely you."

The bear sat down in front of Mani and cleared its throat, as if preparing for a formal introduction. "My name is Ooshaka. I believe you called me?"

Mani was silent. Her mother had explained something about this, but Mani had thought they were just stories—enchanting tales of the animals that had lived in the old snowy world many years before she was born. *There is another world*, she had told her, *filled with life and love and stories. Every human on earth has a guide there. And every human will pass there when their time here is done. The guide you find is the guide you need. It's yours. All your ancestors are there, and one day you will learn what they have to say.*

But Mani hadn't called anyone. And what use did she have for a giant talking polar bear? And weren't they extinct, anyway?

"What is it you want, Mani?" the bear continued gently.

Well, this is easy, thought Mani. What was the thing she wanted most—craved—in the whole world? Without hesitating, she declared, "I want my mother."

As she said the words, a pain ripped through her stomach. She closed her eyes. When she opened them, she was back inside the cave, the mask in her lap, plain and wooden again. All she knew now was it hurt. And, if that pain was hunger, she had to find something to eat.

Chapter 3

Mani's stomach felt like it had turned inside out and was eating itself. And it hurt more than anything she had ever felt before. She shook her head. The snow world she had found behind the mask had filled her mind— the blind-white endless expanse and the talking bear—but had she been dreaming? Hallucinating with hunger? She put the mask back in her bag. Whatever was happening, she needed to think about what she should do next.

She looked at the last jar of *rak-rak*. It was nearly all gone. And there was still no sign of her father returning. She would have to do something. Rules or no rules. The pickled rat might have run out, but she could go out and catch a fresh one, couldn't she? Surely that's what her father would do?

Her thoughts returned helplessly now to those that had been dominating her mind—day and night—as she constantly—obsessively—went over all the things they used to eat, imagining different tastes on her tongue and longing for the sensation of fullness in her tummy. Boiled seal flipper. Caribou stomach. Rabbit tail. And plenty of it. Those nights when everyone would gather round the fire and there would be singing and stories and big plates being handed round and shared. And now she was all alone in the dark with almost nothing left to eat. And that made her want to cry. But she mustn't. Because what if her father came back now, and found her crying?

At the base of the cave, there was water. This water came from somewhere deep and dark in the earth—Mani didn't like to think too much about where exactly—but she knew that it flowed out of the cave to the big river that led to the sea. In the distance, Mani could hear the waterfall where it joined the river. The noise had become familiar and soothing. There was something else out there at least.

But the water inside the cave was dead. Mani had spent long hours staring into it, dipping her hands in, trying to see past the shiny moonlit reflections for signs of life. But it was just clear water that ran through her fingers. She looked out towards the moonlit horizon. Surely not everything had died with the disease? That's why her father had gone out hunting. And there must be stuff growing—wild crowberries to boil and make into jam, and thick ribbons of salty kelp which you could slice off and eat straight away. Mani's stomach grumbled noisily, and tears pricked at her eyes again. But there was her father's voice: *You must not leave the cave.* And, for the first time, Mani started to answer it back: "But I'm hungry," she complained.

Mani was beginning to realize that, if she was going to eat, she would have to go out there. She had no choice. Otherwise, she would starve to death. And her father would return to find her here—a skeleton lying obediently on the sealskin rug. What good would that be?

She pushed her bag with the mask inside it to the back of the cave and clasped the carved whalebone handle of her knife in its holster around her waist. Somehow, just holding it made her feel stronger. She crouched at the cave entrance and stretched out her free hand, feeling a light flutter of wind across her fingertips. She could hear the sound of the waterfall more clearly now, and felt a stuttering of excitement inside.

She placed her bare foot onto the first big rock outside the cave entrance and peered out. The moonlight on the water made the river look like a giant white snake winding forward to the horizon. Everything was still. Mani crouched on the rock and listened.

As she started to climb down the rocks that tumbled out from the cave, she imagined what she would tell her mother if she were here. How proud she would be. *You went out all on your own, to hunt for food?* she would say. And, closing her eyes, she could feel her mother's kiss on her head, the soft warmth of her body.

She squeezed the knife handle harder as she held onto the memory. But then her foot caught on

15

something sharp and she let out a yelp of pain. In the silver moonlight, she could see a dark smear of blood glistening across her big toe. She blinked. But she didn't stop. Instead, she started to move faster, scrambling away from all the emptiness and the loneliness and the hunger.

Chapter 4

As Mani got closer to the waterfall, a light wind picked up and she could feel the cool spray on her face. The noise of thundering water got louder and louder. She carried on down the wet, slippery rocks. They were sharp and dug into the soles of her feet, but eventually gave way to a silty beach. Stopping for a moment, she allowed the cool mud to ooze between her toes and soothe her burning feet.

At the water's edge, she noticed movement—a silver bubbling in the gloomy, muddy shallows. She crouched down to see better. Fly larvae. These would do. She lifted one out between her finger and thumb and put it straight in her mouth and chewed. It popped against her teeth and tasted sweet and salty at the same time, but the mud stuck to her gums and left a fusty, gritty taste. She stepped out deeper into the river and scooped clear water to her lips. Then she lifted a handful of the larvae from the mud and allowed them to swill around in her cupped hands before cramming them all into her mouth. She splashed back to the beach, chewing noisily. Her stomach accepted the bubbling mass gratefully.

Mani looked around her. Down the river was their old village. In the shadows on the opposite bank she could make out some rough steps which someone had made from cut logs. They led up from the grey silty beach to the forbidden path that disappeared into the darkness—the path that led to the *zientzia* and the research station. She had never been up there. She wasn't allowed. It was another of her father's rules. *The cursed place*, he called it. It would only bring bad luck to anyone who was tempted to go there.

Mani became aware of another noise—a gentle rhythmic knocking of what sounded like bone on rock. Her eyes scanned the beach and she was surprised to see a kayak, just like her father's, gently tapping against a dark rock in the shallow water. Her heart leaped. She ran to greet the boat—was her father here? Had he come back at last? Was it his boat? But she couldn't see anyone. With the cool, dark water lapping at her ankles, she ran her hand along the side of the kayak. It was made in the traditional way, with a whalebone frame covered in stretched sealskin. She pressed her cheek against the smooth hide surface. It smelled of animal and the sea and adventure.

Without thinking, she climbed inside and had the feeling she was climbing into the past: she was out on the open water again, with her father, spear raised to strike at the masses of char teeming in the lively water beneath them. And for a moment she thought she could do it, she could go out there today, to the open sea, in the boat, all on her own. But where was he? Where was Tatka?

There was a scuttling sound and the naked pink body of a rat disappeared into the folds of a fur skin lying in the base of the boat, its tail disappearing last like a snake. Mani pulled gently at the fur. She couldn't see the rat, but, under the fur skin, arranged in a neat row, were five strange-looking bones. They were clearly bones, but were not like any Mani had seen before. They were a deep brown-red colour, as if they were dyed or burned, and in the darkness they seemed to pulse with an angry light. Mani pulled the fur skin back some more and found these smaller bones were connected to longer, thicker, red bones, which connected to a red knotty shoulder blade and finally led to the gaping black eye sockets of a human skull. There were fragments of skin still hanging from the bony face and its teeth were gritted in a grotesque grin.

Mani dropped the fur skin and leaped back. She tumbled out of the boat and into the muddy shallows, hauling herself onto the beach, spattering mud and water as she tried to get away. And then she turned and kicked out wildly with her feet, pushing at the boat to get rid of it, get it gone, and she only stopped when it floated away down the river and out of sight. She crawled frantically to the bigger rocks at the back of the beach. Hot tears streamed down her face. In that moment, she wished she'd never left the cave. She wished she'd stayed there with the last of the stinking *rak-rak*, watching the stupid shadows on the wall, and she wished she'd waited, as she was supposed to. Her father's rules were there for a reason—they kept everyone safe. What on earth had she been thinking?

Mani sat and caught her breath, holding her hands over her face and peeping through her fingers to check the boat had gone. But another movement on the opposite side of the river caught her attention now. And there was the sound of a voice.

Mani's hands dropped as she saw the hunched figure of a man—pale and thin—shuffling along the water's edge, holding onto the weeds and roots on the bank for balance. He was muttering to himself, but Mani couldn't make out any words. She watched.

The man was old—older than her father, at least. He wore glasses and had wispy thin hair and a light scraggly beard, which looked scruffy against the smart light-coloured shirt and trousers he wore. *Zientzia*, Mani thought. A science-man. She didn't move.

He was carrying a big plastic container, and now he bent down, muttering and complaining as he held it submerged in the water. After a while, he heaved it out and screwed on a lid, then he turned and climbed back up the log steps on the riverbank.

Mani craned to see where he went, but he had disappeared. She stared after him. So, her father had been wrong. Wrong about one thing, at least. Not *everyone* had died. They weren't alone, after all.

"Ooshaka! Ooshaka!" called Mani. "Where are you? I've come back!"

She was walking quickly over squeaky snow and shouting the polar bear's name. There was nothing but whiteness as far as the eye could see.

"Ooshaka! Ooshaka!" Her voice was strong—defiant, even.

She became aware of the polar bear next to her. It was walking in time with her, keeping pace. The faster she went, the faster the bear went, matching her step for step.

"Hey—slow down a bit, will you?" the bear said eventually.

Mani stopped suddenly and turned, her hands on her hips. "Where are they then, Ooshaka? Where are all the dead people?"

Ooshaka held her gaze, but didn't answer.

"Aren't they supposed to be here? The ancestors, the *dead* people…? Can't I talk to them?" She stretched her arms out and spun around. The horizon blurred into endless white. There was no line where the earth stopped and the sky began. And there was no one to be seen.

"Where are they?" She fired the question again at Ooshaka. Then she threw back her head and shouted, "Where are yooouuuuu?" Her voice echoed across the empty landscape, like a wolf's howl, and when she stopped, it carried on without her.

21

There was still no answer. Not from Ooshaka. Not from anyone. And the sky just returned her lonely cry. Mani fell on her knees and stared into the snow. It was no good. It was all a lie. There was no one here. She must surely be dreaming, or dying, or something. And one thing was certain. She wouldn't find her mother here. She was all alone.

"Well," Ooshaka finally spoke. "I don't usually need to explain it…The people who come here usually know…and we…well, we just guide…sort of…"

Mani looked up. "But I want to see them. I want to meet my ancestors. The ones my mother told me about. I want to meet the dead people. I can't just be here on my own. There must be someone. *Something.*"

And she stopped and dug her hands into the frozen ground and held them there until they started to ache and she could bear it no more. She looked up again.

"I want to see my mother, Ooshaka. Tell me. Is she here?"

She felt her stomach lurch and growl. The wretched hunger. She could never escape it. She closed her eyes and bent over. It hurt. And Ooshaka's voice, when she heard it again, sounded very far away.

"Go back, Mani. And when you're ready we can look for her. Together. You and me—we have things to do. You have lots to learn. Come back and see me soon…"

And the bear's voice died away gently, like an echo in a deep well, until once again all was silent and dark.

Chapter 5

Mani didn't know how long she'd been walking—was it five minutes or five hours since she had left the cave and waded across the river in search of the science-man she had seen there? She could see the research station in the distance, but it didn't seem to be getting any closer. The wind was loud and violent and tore across the plain, whipping up whirlwinds of dust. It punched her around the face and stuck fists in her ears so she couldn't hear properly. Every so often she tripped and the rocks dug into her bruised and cut bare feet. The ground seemed to be dipping and rising beneath her. She stopped for a moment and gulped for breath.

Stay away. That's what her father would say. Mani knew the rule. They'd all known it. It was unwritten. Unspoken too, mostly, except for when her father took her to one side to spell it out. Some of the kids broke it, and they came back from the research station with stuff. Weird food, usually. Once, someone had brought back an old phone and they'd watched cartoons on it in secret, until the battery died. Her father had never found out.

And now she was breaking the rules. She was on her way to find the science-man she'd seen at the river. She'd thought about it all that night. But it was her hunger now that had to be obeyed.

There it was—all the way across the plain—squatting between the two mountains like a giant insect: the science-men's research station. Was it getting any closer?

It was still dark, but something was giving on the horizon. A hint that the sun was making its return after the long month of polar darkness. There was a push of orange, and the insect-building was briefly silhouetted, giant and black, against the faintly glowing sky.

She *was* getting closer. She could see now that the insect was made up of three parts, or pods—head, belly, and tail—all connected by a floating walkway. In the middle pod—its belly—an orange light flickered. A sign, Mani thought. She walked faster.

She headed for the light, finally arriving at the foot of a metal staircase. It was rusting, red paint peeling back in cracks and curls, and one of the steps had broken and was hanging loose. Everything swayed and rattled and clanked in the wind.

The staircase led up to a heavy metal door. At the top, the wind was so strong, it felt like it might throw her off. She grasped the door handle and wrenched it open. Inside was a small porch. And then—*woomp*—the heavy door slammed shut behind her. It was suddenly, deafeningly, silent. The rattling wind was gone, and all Mani could hear was the sound of her own shaky breathing.

The next door had a window through which Mani could see the source of the light. She pressed her face to the glass. There was a table and a candle. And a man. The same science-man she'd seen down at the river. Still shuffling around. Still talking to himself.

Mani watched. The science-man was busy. Next to the candle was a blue flame, and, on top of that, a steaming pan. The science-man lifted the pan and poured its contents into a bowl.

Then came the smell. Warm and savoury. It teased around the edges of the door and under Mani's nose, creeping down to her stomach, causing it to lurch and flip. *Food.*

Without thinking, Mani pushed at the door, which opened easily. She stepped forward into the room and heard it swing shut behind her.

The science-man looked up, the pan still in his hand. And Mani saw it straight away. *He has it*, she thought. The disease. The one her mother got. The one that killed everyone. That was how it started. With the eyes.

Mani stared. The science-man's eyes were just like her mother's had been before she died. And everyone had been the same. Not so much glowing in the dark, but

25

more fizzing and crackling with tiny thread-like lightning strikes, lines of what looked like electricity pulsing out from the pupil. Like mini-electric storms all contained within the globe of the eye. This was how her mother's eyes had looked. Until the lids had finally closed.

The science-man stared at Mani, his eyes sparking electric in the darkness, making it hard to read any expression in his face. Mani stumbled back towards the door but fell onto the hard floor. Neither moved. They just stayed, looking at each other.

Then the science-man, still holding Mani with his electric gaze, placed the pan down and reached out to pick up the bowl. He held it towards Mani and nodded. He said something that Mani couldn't quite make out. But his voice was gentle—friendly, even. Mani stayed on the ground and didn't move.

The science-man edged forward and gently lowered the bowl onto the floor. He shuffled back to the table. When he was at a safe distance, Mani crawled towards the bowl, grabbing it with one hand and scrabbling back to the door. Its contents—broth and a noodly mixture—slopped messily. Without taking her eyes off the man, Mani scooped handfuls of the scalding mixture into her mouth. It slid and scorched its way down into her stomach. And when she couldn't pick up any more with her hand, she tipped the bowl to her mouth, draining every last bit. She closed her eyes and felt her tummy fill and the warmth expand out through her heart and limbs.

26

When she opened her eyes, for a moment she was lost, and she couldn't remember where she'd come or why. But here she was still, inside the belly of the insect. And there was the science-man still, staring at her.

Mani dropped the bowl suddenly. It clattered onto the concrete floor. She had to get out. As her hunger faded, her father's voice returned inside her head: *Stay away.* And, without a word, she turned and ran as fast as she could, heaving open the heavy door with all her strength, down the steps onto the dusty plain, and back across the river to the cave, all the time chanting under her breath: "Please come home, please come home, please come home, Tatka."

Chapter 6

There was no question about going back the next day. What else could Mani do? She had to eat. And there was food there. "I am starving," she explained to no one, as she ran across the plain, her tummy growling impatiently.

The sun was nibbling at the horizon again—each day it would get a little bigger—but, for now, just a peel of orange rose briefly behind the giant insect, illuminating it only for a moment, before dropping away and casting the world into darkness again.

This time, when Mani pushed the door to the belly-pod open, she found it was empty. The same candle was flickering on the table at the far end of the room. It looked small and shaky across the open space and clean white shiny floor.

Workbenches and high stools were positioned at regular intervals. At the nearest bench, Mani could see someone had set a bowl and spoon and two small cartons. She climbed up onto the stool nearest the bowl—her feet dangled above the ground and she had to hold onto the side of the bench to steady herself. The rest of the room seemed to disappear around her as she now examined the two plain-white cartons.

The first one rattled when she picked it up. She shook it and then held it to her nose; it smelled sweet. She tore open the card and inner bag. Inside were hard round nuggets which she emptied into the bowl. She picked one up and bit it. It was like a small rock in her mouth, but there was a pleasing sugariness on her tongue. The second carton had a plastic spout on top and made a sloshing sound when she shook it. She pressed open the spout. Drops of milk splattered out. She tipped it into the bowl and stirred the mixture with the spoon and then shovelled it into her mouth. It sogged and slid down easily. This was good. She gobbled down more of the sweet slush.

After a while, she became aware of the door at the opposite end of the room opening, and in walked the science-man. He stopped and watched Mani. Perhaps she should have done something else—perhaps she should have just left, or said she was sorry for coming again uninvited and taking food that wasn't hers to take—but the hunger drove her on and she ate faster.

She couldn't see much of the science-man's face— just his eyes, which flashed white and purple and red electricity through the space between them. Had he

29

been watching all along? Had he laid the food out for Mani? Or had he planned to eat it himself?

The science-man nodded his head in Mani's direction. This seemed like a good sign—a sort of *Yes*—so Mani carried on eating. But when the science-man took a step forward, Mani froze. A dribble of milk ran down her chin, but she didn't dare move to wipe it off.

What did he want? He'd better not come near—he was sick.

The science-man cleared his throat. When he spoke, his voice sounded thin and weak and tired. "My name is Dr Leopold MacKintosh." He held out his hand. Mani flinched and wobbled on the high stool. The science-man stepped back and raised both hands. Maybe he was saying *It's OK*, but maybe he was saying *You're not welcome*—Mani couldn't tell. When he spoke again, it was louder. "But you can call me Leo."

Mani thought for a moment. This was friendly. So, she still had time. Reaching for the box, she poured more nuggets into the bowl. But the science-man's words hung in the air between them. *My name is…* Names? Mani thought. They never had *names*. They were just *zientzia*. Foreigners. Invaders. Science-men. They didn't belong here. But this one—he had a name. *Leo-science-man*. And Mani could call him *Leo*?

Mani looked at him. *Leo*. She saw how his eyes flashed and crackled in the dark and she thought of the disease. It had taken Matka away. Perhaps Leo-science-man would die soon too, Mani thought. He would be just like the others. Would he pass into the world beyond this? Would she search for him behind the mask too?

Mani knew she had to keep her distance, as her father had told her, or she would catch it. Perhaps the science-man was waiting here alone, preparing to die? A feeling of sadness wrapped around her, like a rope pulling her down, but something inside her made her speak.

Her voice sounded different in the insect-room. It was so long since she'd spoken out loud that her voice rattled like pebbles in a tin, echoing around the clean shiny surfaces. But she said, slowly and carefully, "My name is Mani." Then she pointed with her finger into her chest and nodded, and said again, quite clearly, "Mani."

Chapter 7

Routines are good. They make you feel safe. You know what will happen next. And so now a new routine formed. Each day, as soon as the owl came to perch at the cave entrance, Mani left again to see the science-man and get more food.

Her visits were getting longer, her stomach fuller, and when she returned to the dark and dusty familiarity of the cave each evening, her father's voice in her head was getting quieter. The cave entrance still stared emptily back at her as she approached it, but it felt like a new space in her head was opening up, filled with the bright, shiny world that she had found inside the insect-building.

It was different in there. It was exciting. It smelled clean and soapy. There were cupboards and chairs, and tables with shiny tops. And there was stuff inside the cupboards—not just food, but other things too: machines and equipment.

The floor underneath her bare feet was kind and smooth, not like the dirty rough rubble of the cave.

The science-man—Leo—seemed happy for her to explore. But still there were rules. Always rules. One day, he led her out of the belly of the insect and along a narrow windowless corridor into the "head" room. Before he pushed open the door, he turned back to look at her. "Don't touch." He spoke firmly and wagged his finger. "Don't touch *anything* unless I say." And he held Mani with a long, crackling stare.

Although the sun was making more of an appearance every day now, it was still far from full daylight, so Leo lit candles, which he placed on a large table in the centre of the circular room. Each time Mani reached out to examine something, Leo barked "Don't touch!" and wagged his finger. But she was allowed to *look*. And Leo stood by the door as Mani walked around the room peering at all the strange equipment, her hands glued to her sides. There were rows and rows of computer screens, all switched off. And there were other machines and pieces of equipment with buttons and levers and screens and switches. Mani fought the urge to reach out and press and jab and pull things, but it all looked broken anyway. Screens were darkened and plugs had been removed. Everywhere were wires with frayed ends where they had been cut. Everything was dark and lifeless.

There was one thing Mani *was* allowed to touch. Leo showed her a pile of notebooks and motioned to her that it was OK to take a look. They sat down at a table. Mani picked up the top one and, when there was no objection from Leo, opened it and flipped through the pages. There were scribbles and notes and symbols that she didn't understand. Leo turned to a fresh page in one of the books and produced a pen. He looked at Mani and slid them across the table to her. Then he spoke. Mani had got used to his voice. It was soft but clipped and business-like, and he spoke slowly, saying each word precisely.

"Where is your mother, Mani?"

An impossible question. It was all Mani had been asking herself since Matka had died, because she didn't really believe she could have gone. Even if she had known how to answer, she couldn't have said the words out loud. Because that would make it real. And she was still looking for her, so it couldn't be real.

Leo repeated, "Where is your mother?"

Mother. Matka. Where are you? a voice whispered in Mani's head, and she felt a cold swoosh of frozen air rush over her. Mani shook herself. She stared at the blank page, then looked back at Leo. Picking up the pen, she drew two long shapes—eyes—and from their pupils she tore jagged lightning bolts into the paper. She closed her own eyes to stop the tears forming.

Leo's voice continued gently, "And your father?"

There was a pause. Mani opened her eyes. *Father. Tatka.* She looked out of the window. *Are you ever coming back?* Mani looked back at Leo. She still couldn't form an answer in words, so she scrawled a second picture, this time of a fish, and pointed outside.

34

"Gone to find food? Catch fish?" Leo asked. "To eat?"

Mani nodded, and they both stared out through the windows into the thick empty darkness.

Leo stood up. "Don't go anywhere!" he said, and he disappeared through the door.

After a while, Mani heard his footsteps clanking back along the metal walkway. The door swung open and he appeared holding something in his hand. He placed a flat round object on the table and stepped back. Mani lifted the object and turned it over. It was a mirror.

She peered at her reflection, but it wasn't the dirty, thinner, older face looking back at her that was the shock, nor the long, matted hair and ripped T-shirt she barely recognized. It was the eyes that she saw flashing back at her—firing lightning and electricity from her pupils— that caused her to slam the mirror down on the table and fall backwards.

She looked up at Leo. She had the disease too? She had caught it? Like her mother had? So why wasn't she already dead?

"Am I sick, Ooshaka? Am I dying?" Mani's hair fluttered as Ooshaka breathed in and out. "And where is she, Ooshaka? Where is my mother?"

"You'll find her, Mani; you just have to look."

Ooshaka was lying opposite Mani. Either side of them, the frozen plains extended, endlessly clean and white. Ooshaka rested her head on her huge front paws. Mani lay opposite her, on her tummy too, her chin resting on her hands. Their noses were almost touching.

"Tell me about her, Mani."

Mani looked into Ooshaka's deep black eyes as she thought. Then she rolled onto her back and looked up into the sky. She felt Ooshaka do the same. The ice creaked beneath them as the bear moved, and trembled as she relaxed her bulk in the new position. They watched a single cloud pass lazily above them.

Mani closed her eyes. And then she saw her. First, her smile—broad and twinkling. Then, her skin— smooth mostly, with tiny hairline wrinkles at the corners of her eyes, which deepened with her smile. And her laugh. She could hear her laugh. Light and melodic. Like water running over pebbles. And she could see the wisps of dark hair on her forehead that she was always tucking away. And her nose—straight and slightly too big for her face.

Mani opened her eyes suddenly. It was like she was really there. High above, an eagle circled. Mani watched it. Something about its size, the ease with which it sliced through the sky, and its massive, feathered wings made her heart beat faster.

"She was strong," she said, her eyes fixed on the bird.

The eagle was getting lower in the sky with each turn. Mani could see the soft white down of its belly and the long, black feathers at the tips of its wings that splayed out like fingers. As it got closer to the ground, it

36

started to beat its wings with powerful sweeps. Its fanned tail moved up and down with each beat. The sound was like a whisper, a strong out-breath, getting ever closer.

"She was adventurous."

The bird was so low now, Mani could feel its shadow across her face and body. She could feel the wind of each wingbeat. She could see its yellow talons tucked into its belly, and the occasional flash of a sharp claw.

"She was fearless."

Finally, it landed silently beside them on the ice. Mani looked at its face as it surveyed the land protectively. Its eyes were fierce, as if daring the world to come and challenge it.

Mani felt safe. This was what had been missing since her mother had gone.

The eagle blinked slowly and, as it turned to look at Mani, the black and tan feathers around its eyes seemed to gather, almost like laughter lines. Its beak, a little too big for its face, was nevertheless strong and noble.

She was here.

"And I love her," Mani finally said.

Chapter 8

The next day, when Mani visited Leo, she stood squarely in front of him and asked, "Am I going to die?"

Leo, who was in the middle of opening the day's ration of noodles, froze. He stared back at Mani and swallowed. He placed the half-opened packet on the table. "It's time we had a talk," he said. "A proper think. We both have questions."

It was dark outside and Leo lit a candle. He pulled up two chairs to the workbench and placed an open notebook and pen in front of them. He poured two glasses of milk and carefully placed two biscuits on a plate.

They sat down together. Mani drank the milk noisily, her eyes on Leo all the time. She stuffed a dry biscuit into her mouth, spraying crumbs as she ate.

Leo pressed the pen against his chin, and then tapped it on the workbench. "You ask an interesting question, Mani. It's a question I've been asking myself. And I can't answer. When so many have died of this disease—" he pointed at his eyes— "why haven't I? And now you? It's a puzzle. Perhaps we can help each other work it out?"

Mani nodded. "Can I have this?" she asked, pointing to the second biscuit.

Leo pushed the plate towards her and carried on. "Black and white thinking is what we need. Scientific observation. What can we see? And what can we understand from that?"

Mani's mouth was crammed full of dry biscuit now and she couldn't speak.

"So, let's start at the beginning. What do we know?" Leo drew a big number one on the page. He looked at Mani. "Come on, let's make a scientist of you. What do we know for certain?"

Mani swallowed and looked back at Leo's electric eyes. She thought about her own eyes, and her mother's, and all the other people who had had the same eyes. They had all died. "We're sick," said Mani quietly, wiping her mouth on her arm. Except, the strange thing was, Mani didn't feel sick. And she certainly didn't feel as if she was dying.

"Excellent," said Leo eventually, smiling at Mani. "Excellent observation." And, next to the number one, he wrote down: *We are sick*. "But," He turned his head to look at Mani. "And this is the difficult bit. How do we know?"

Mani frowned. Wasn't it obvious? She pressed her finger into the crumbs on the table. "Our eyes are...like *this*," she said, pointing her crumb-loaded finger up to her face before delivering the crumbs to her mouth.

"Indeed, indeed." Leo clicked the pen with his thumb. "So...yes...to answer your first question: the outlook for us isn't good, because we have both seen many with this disease—with eyes like ours—die. But that isn't the end of the story, is it? Because here we are. We aren't dead." Leo forced brightness into his voice. "So...what else?" he asked.

Mani shrugged. She took a gulp of milk.

"Well...let's think...What did your father tell you?" Leo probed.

Mani could remember the day it happened. Her father had come back from talking to the science-men. Her mother was in the makeshift hospital at the school, along with all the others. Mani had been told to wait at home. She had never seen her father so angry. His face was red and he shook with rage. He'd shouted about the *meddling zientzia* and had sent Mani to her room, slamming the door behind her, while he and the last few from the village continued a furious debate.

Later, at the hospital, Mani had watched through the window as her father knelt at her mother's bed and wept. Her father never cried. Mani hadn't understood what was happening. If she had, perhaps she would have been angry too.

40

She looked at Leo. "My father said that the science-men brought it. And then everyone died. It was your fault. And that made him mad."

Leo nodded slowly. "Yes, yes, indeed. A disease. Highly contagious. But now you're going off track a little…You're forgetting—science is about observing; you must only state what you see. And your father—well, he was 'mad', as you say, and quite rightly—so emotion would then…well…colour his judgement?"

Leo waited for a reaction, but Mani didn't say anything.

"As scientists, we need to be totally free from emotion. We must only state what we can see in front of us. Blame won't help."

"But…," Mani mumbled, recalling what her father had said. "You dug it up. You brought it out—it was so deep, so ancient, you had no right to disturb it. So it *is* your fault."

"Well…no…but…," said Leo, staring at the page in front of him. "Yes, we lifted it out from the earth…but it was already half out. Have you heard about the snow and ice, Mani? Many years before your time?"

Mani fidgeted on her seat next to Leo. Of course she knew about the ice!

"Well, the rock had been buried in the ice for thousands of years. And, as the ice melted, all those years ago, it was slowly pushed to the surface, and that's how we discovered it. The earth pushed it out—we didn't dig for it. The disease would have come out eventually." Leo

41

stood up now and went to the window. "And it looked so different—like nothing I'd ever seen before. Its colour... its luminescence...a red, fiery beauty in it...We thought we could change the world with it." He turned back to Mani. "We're scientists. We had to examine it properly. Observe it. Ask questions. As we're doing now."

He sat down and picked up the pen again. "But, I think...yes...we can add a second fact to our list." He drew a large number two in the notebook and beside it wrote: *We have the disease that came from the red rock.*

"Now, let's get on." Leo brushed his hand over the page, as if cleaning away any emotion that had threatened to cloud his thoughts. "So, what do we know about this sickness? What do we know *for sure*? What have we seen? How is it affecting us?"

But Mani had said all she knew. She didn't feel any different. It was just that everyone around her had disappeared—and her whole world had slipped away almost overnight. What she wanted to know was—would she die next?

"Well, let's summarize what we've got," Leo said eventually. He wrote a number three in a careful script on the notepad and spoke slowly and deliberately as he continued the list:

3. What we know about the disease:
a) it came out of a red rock we pulled from the earth.
b) it is unlike anything we have ever seen before.
c) after infection: certain death.

42

This final point hung in the air between them. Mani looked up at Leo.

"But we have some time," Leo added, and he scrawled a question mark next to the word *death*, "because I have taken precautions. There is one important thing that I know now, that wasn't known before—that your father can't have known." He leaned forward towards Mani now and wagged his finger. "Electricity," he said.

And, as if to underline it, he repeated, "E-LEC-TRICITY."

Mani was confused. What did electricity have to do with anything?

Leo put the pen down. His voice lowered. "This is very important. You must listen. There is one thing I know with absolute certainty about the disease: it feeds on electricity."

Was this why Leo was living in darkness, with only candlelight? Was this why all the equipment in the insect-building was broken or with cut wires?

Leo continued, "This disease…it's living…it lives inside us. And it feeds on the small electric current that all healthy humans have naturally inside them. That is what it is doing right now."

Leo pointed at his eyes, and then at Mani's.

"But," he continued, wagging his finger in the air, "the disease is greedy. It wants more. And it hunts down electricity wherever it can. So, if we go near any electrical equipment or plugs or lightning—*anything*—we are doomed. Because the disease will suck it all in and grow

43

and destroy us from the inside. The more electricity it gets, the faster it grows and the quicker the end is. Burned alive. From the inside out." Leo shivered. "And that will be our only mercy: death is quick." He looked at the notebook. "So, we have another point for our list."

d) the disease is alive—it feeds on electricity: stay away at all costs.

Leo set the pen down. "To answer your question: yes—I believe we are dying, but slowly, and if we can avoid electricity, we will have more time. How much, I don't know." He stood up. "But I intend to use whatever time I have to try and understand it. And what I learn will be my gift—my legacy, as a scientist—to the world. I hope that whoever finds my notes—" he tapped the notebook— "will make use of them after I have gone. And they will find a cure. And my life and death will not be in vain." He turned to look at Mani now. "Will you help me?"

Without waiting for an answer, he walked to a cupboard at the edge of the room.

"Our next step is to look more closely at it." He opened the cupboard and pulled out a strange-looking machine. "And there's only one way we can do that. There is one thing we both have that can help us."

He carried the machine back to the workbench.

"Blood," he declared, staring at Mani.

Mani was tired. She was lying across Ooshaka's chest, her head nestled between the bear's front legs. It was so comfortable.

She was thinking of her old bed at home. Soft and warm, with feather pillows and a cosy duvet. She snuggled deeper into Ooshaka's downy tummy fur. It felt just like this. She could see her bed. At the head, in front of the window, her mother had hung the dreambell. They had made it together, bending the wood to make a spiral frame, attaching long threads of wool and tying on beads and dried flowers and soft feathers. This, her mother had explained, would catch the good dreams and drop them softly into her sleeping head. And Mani had only ever had good dreams sleeping below the dreambell.

Mani felt Ooshaka's bulk shift beneath her and she sat up straighter. The bear was looking up into the sky. Mani looked up too. Above, way up high, the eagle was circling. It drew huge expansive circles across the whole blue sky. Mani leaned into Ooshaka and pushed her neck back as far as she could to keep watching. A single, soft, downy feather fell from the sky in ever-decreasing circles. Mani and Ooshaka watched its progress, closer and closer, until finally it landed in Mani's lap. She picked it up and twirled it between her thumb and forefinger. *Dreambell*, Mani thought. Matka. And she looked back up at the distant eagle.

Then, from far away, came a soulful howl. It was a sad sound and it made Mani ache inside. A wolf's call from somewhere distant. And it was calling her. She fought the urge to get up from her comfy bed on Ooshaka's chest and tramp out into the emptiness to find where it was coming from. She buried her face deep into Ooshaka's fur, her hand squeezed around the feather. She wanted to make this moment last longer. It was so comfortable and nice and warm.

But there it was again.

The howl.

Something was calling.

And Mani knew she couldn't stay in the same place forever. She knew, this time, she would have to go.

Chapter 9

Blood. It turned out that blood always looked the same. Whether it was from a seal, a fish, a human… always the same. From the outside, at least.

Mani stared at the small orb of red blood on Leo's finger. It was tiny and perfect and shiny. She watched as he crushed it between two small rectangles of glass.

He then slid the glass onto a small tray beneath the machine that had what looked like binoculars on top. Beneath the tray a small flame inside a glass case was burning. He put a small round plaster on the tip of his finger, but it peeled away immediately. "Drat," he muttered, scrunching up the plaster and wiping his finger across his white shirt. A faint trail of red smeared down from the collar over his chest.

Leo looked up at Mani and pointed with his other hand to the machine.

"This is called a *microscope*," he said. "Have you seen one before? It's for looking at small things." He squinted one eye and pinched his finger and thumb almost together, peering through the tiny gap to illustrate *small*. "And this," he added, pointing to the slide and then to his shirt, "is my blood."

Mani nodded.

Leo pressed his face to the eyepieces of the binoculars. He seemed to stay there for a long while. Then he looked up and stared into the distance and shook his head, before bending to look at the slide again. "It's odd," he muttered, and then turned to look at Mani.

Up close, Mani could see the strangeness in Leo's diseased eyes more clearly. The tiny lightning bolts that crackled from the dark centre were shooting out smaller branches of lightning, and each smaller branch gave out more branches, and it was like lightning on lightning on lightning, each time smaller and smaller and smaller. It made his eyes look like they were fizzing, and even *moving* with the energy contained inside.

"Do you want a look?" Leo asked. "See if you can make sense of it?" He shifted off his stool and invited Mani to sit. "This is my blood. It's sick blood. Diseased blood. It's not normal."

Mani climbed up. She bent her head over the binocular eyepieces, as she'd seen Leo do, and peered in. It turned out that blood wasn't always red. Not when you looked closely. Or at least Leo's "sick blood" wasn't. It seemed to be made of millions of tiny luminescent fiery cells. They were hexagon-shaped, and they were in constant movement, passing quickly and jerkily into any space they could find. And, just like Leo's eyes, they too were shooting out tiny lightning strikes. But, without the eyeball to contain them, they seemed to be able to reach out further, losing the jaggedness of the lightning shape. Instead, they looked like thread-thin luminescent fishing lines being thrown out in all directions, trying to hook something, but each time they were hauled back in, empty.

Mani glanced up at Leo, and then at the red smear on his shirt. It didn't make sense. The blood looked red and shiny, from the outside. But inside was this frantic light show.

"Do you want to see yours?" Leo said. From a box beside the table, he took a small cellophane packet and ripped open the top. He pulled out a needle and, before removing the cap, mimed pressing it against his finger with a gentle stabbing motion. "Like I did. Just a scratch." He handed it to Mani.

Mani took the cap off and pressed the end of the needle into the fleshy part of her fingertip, just as she'd seen Leo do—it didn't hurt at all. She watched the small orb of red appear on her finger, holding it up to her eyes and staring into it. Yes. Blood. The same as everyone else.

Leo placed a glass slide on the table in front of her and showed her how to press her finger onto it. Mani squashed the tiny blood ball into the glass and then wiped her finger on her T-shirt, just as she'd seen Leo do.

Leo reached across and took the slide. He slotted it under the microscope next to his own. "Let's see, now," he muttered, looking down through the eyepieces. But this time he didn't lift his head. He stayed bent over the slide. His breathing became heavier and quicker, and his neck looked damp. "This is very strange...very strange indeed." He stood up and gestured for Mani to take a look.

Mani peered into the binoculars.

"Do you see?" asked Leo, behind her.

Mani did see. Her blood was different. There were none of the threads of light and none of the movement. In Mani's blood, the hexagon cells were luminescent, like Leo's, but they were fixed in place—like in a beehive. Nothing was moving. Mani's blood looked still—as if it was complete.

Mani heard her stomach grumble. She didn't know what any of this stuff about their blood meant, but she understood her tummy.

Leo pulled the microscope across and looked into it again. "Think," he muttered to himself, his hands squeezing into fists on the workbench. "Observe," he commanded himself. "What could it mean?" He looked up at Mani and stared into her eyes, lost in thought.

"Can we eat now?" Mani asked.

"Eat?" Leo jumped. "Yes...Yes, indeed." He shuffled over to the door, where he had left a large plastic container, muttering all the time to himself, "Think... think...Why the difference? *Why?*" He bent to pick up the container and shook it. "Drat!" he exploded. "We've run out of water." He looked over at the microscope and then at Mani. "I'll have to fill up at the river. Wait here. Don't go anywhere. I'll be quick. We've found something important…We need to look at it more…compare it with normal blood too, if we can." He waved the empty container in the air. "But, we'll have tea first, and then back to work!"

As he was leaving, Leo put his hand on the door and paused. He turned back. "Remember—vitally important—if we're going to get anywhere, we need *time*. So—do *not* touch anything. You know why. *E-lec-tricity.* Stay safe." And there was the stern face again, and the finger wagging and pointing around at the equipment in the lab. With one last lingering look at the microscope, he was gone.

Mani watched him through the window. The dark plain outside was lit by an almost-full moon. Leo seemed tiny as he scuttled across the dusty flats to the river. The wind was tearing across sideways as usual and, as he disappeared into the distance, he looked like a fleck of black dust on a silver cloud that might be blown away at any moment.

Chapter 10

Waiting. Mani was always *waiting.* She had been *waiting* for her father. Now she was *waiting* for Leo. Would anyone ever come back? She slammed her hand down on the table and her fingers stung. Something had to happen soon. And not just this nonsense about blood. Just to end the *waiting.* *Waiting* for the world to return to normal. *Waiting* for her old life to come back.

What if Leo didn't come back? Just like her father hadn't? What if she was left here in this place? And what exactly *was* this place? The insect-building had become sort-of familiar—she'd been here so many times now—but, as she thought about it, she realized there was one section she hadn't been in at all: the third room at the end, the insect's tail. She knew the middle bit, the belly—it was the biggest room, where Leo prepared food and they ate. Then there was this room, the head, which was a little smaller—this was where the interesting equipment was, where Leo worked and Mani watched. But the third room, at the other end—Mani hadn't been in there at all. And Leo hadn't invited her.

What was she waiting for?

When she pushed the door to the third room open, she could see straight away it was different from the other two rooms. It probably wasn't much smaller, but it seemed so because it was divided into a series of sleeping pods—small bedrooms that opened into the central chamber. Each had a bed, a cupboard, and a small circular-shaped window through which moonlight beamed like torchlight. A metal stairway led up to a second level with a second row of identical pods.

Most of the beds were stripped bare, and the cupboards were open and empty. But one was different from the rest. The bed was covered in rumpled sheets and blankets. There were books piled on the small table, beside the stub of an almost-burned-through candle. As she got closer, Mani could see that, alongside the books and blackened candle, there was a single photo in a frame.

She sat down on the bed. It gave way beneath her with such an incredible softness that she felt like gentle arms had scooped her up and were cradling her. She'd spent so long sleeping on the rough floor of the cave, with only a sealskin separating her from the dirty rubble, that this comfort felt otherworldly. She lay down and felt her head engulfed by the soft pillow.

She closed her eyes, expecting to feel sleepy. But she wasn't. She was wide awake. Actually, it felt odd. This was someone else's bed, moulded to someone else's shape, with someone else's smell, and someone else's things. She didn't belong here.

Her eyes snapped open and she jerked her head to the side. She looked at the photo, which was lit blue-white in the glow of the moon. It was a man and a woman and a girl—about Mani's age.

She sat up and swung her legs round, dropping down from the bed and opening the cupboard. She crouched down and peered in. There were a few more belongings inside, including a mirror like the one Leo had brought to her. She picked it up and held it close to her face. She'd forgotten how her eyes were different now. She didn't worry about them, because she couldn't see them, and she didn't feel any different anyway. But they were just like Leo's—and those of everyone else who had had the disease and died.

She set the mirror down and continued to investigate the contents of the cupboard. An old phone. Forgetting everything Leo had said, Mani picked it up and pressed a few buttons—but it was dead, like all the computers and equipment in this place. There was something else: a black and cylindrical object, right at the back. Mani reached in and pulled it out. There was a switch on the side, which she slid to *on*.

The room was transformed in light. A surge of fear rattled through Mani and she felt cold and hot at the same time. Electricity. *Don't touch anything*, Leo had said. She fumbled with the torch and slid the switch to *off*. She paused, the torch in her hand. But nothing had happened to her. The disease hadn't taken over her body like Leo had said it would. She still felt fine. And a switch is a switch and needs to be pressed, so she slid it on again.

The beam of light—so long absent from her world—was a relief. In the small sleeping pod, she could see texture and colour, and the light dug into corners, showing them to be pleasingly empty and not teeming with fearful possibilities. Mani swung the light around the room and what had looked flat and grey was now colour—and she could see that the walls were painted blue and the woollen blankets on the bed were red and orange. Eventually, the beam of light settled on the photo.

Mani picked it up. She could see, now, that the man in the photo was, in fact, Leo. A much younger Leo, without a beard, but most noticeably with normal eyes. The girl was in the centre, sandwiched between Leo and the woman. And they were all smiling—laughing—into the camera. In that moment, Mani could almost feel she was that girl—between her own mother and father, their arms pulling her in and smiling into the future that had ended so suddenly.

Then came the shock. A bolt—a jolt—something from outside flew at her, knocking her sideways. A whooshing sound powered through her head, and she fell to the floor heavily. There was a strange sensation deep inside her—something snapping, like a huge elastic band pinging—causing her whole body to jolt. The torch flew from her hands and landed on the ground, rolling across to the far wall. Mani lay motionless, still looking at the beam of light, which now created a series of circles radiating out over the blue paintwork.

"Stupid child," a voice she almost didn't recognize rasped.

She rolled her head to the side. It was Leo. He was lying on the ground next to her.

"Were you not listening to anything I said? I told you not to touch anything…and especially not—are you mad?—electricity." Then, more softly: "Are you OK?"

Mani couldn't feel her body or move her arms or legs. It was like they weren't there. She could only move her head from side to side. She looked at Leo, who lay on the ground next to her, apparently paralysed too, and then back at the torch.

But there was something different about Leo.

Something had changed.

Leo's eyes had gone back to normal.

Chapter 11

Leo was very excited. He paced around the sleeping pod. Mani had recovered a little—her body felt cold and full of pins and needles, but after a while she was able to sit cross-legged on the floor. Her head moved from side to side as she watched Leo pacing back and forth. He was waving his arms around and talking fast. Non-stop talking.

"My eyes…," he kept muttering, but he never finished the sentence. "I'm better?" he repeated over and over, pointing at his eyes, which were no longer electric but a soft brown colour. He held the mirror up to his face. "I'm free," He switched the torch on and off repeatedly to prove it. *I'm safe, do you see?* he seemed to be saying in his head. The disease had somehow left his body.

But Mani's eyes had not changed. They were crackling and fizzing as much as ever, if not more. Yet she had been able to use the torch with no ill effect.

"How could that be?" Leo kept asking. "What does it mean? Why does it not kill you—the electricity and the sickness—like it killed the others? And why am I better?"

Something big had happened, there was no doubt about that. And Leo thought he knew *what* it was, "But *why*? And *how*?" he kept asking, raising his arms to the ceiling and occasionally bending to stare intensely into Mani's eyes, then peering at his own in the mirror, before resuming his pacing around the pod.

In the moment they had touched, Mani had felt a jolt, a bolt, a giant shock, a ping, a mighty snap inside her. She couldn't really explain this to Leo. Not in words. But Leo tried to describe what *he* had felt. And it was different.

"It was a pulling. Like something being drawn from me," he said, miming pulling a rope from his stomach. "Something left my body. And then it was clear and calm. Normal! Back to being me!" he beamed.

When he had come back from the river with the water, he had found Mani holding the torch—and he had flown at her, to save her from the lethal electricity, knocking the torch from her hands. But Mani was unharmed.

"But you still have the sickness," Leo kept saying, looking at Mani's eyes. "And nothing electric should be safe for you. Not even a torch."

It was true. Mani had been able to hold the torch and switch it on and off, and it had made no difference at all. The disease had not taken over.

It seemed that Mani was different in some way. Leo handed her the torch now to prove it and Mani shone the beam back at Leo's face.

"See? You're safe!" exclaimed Leo, squinting into the light. "But you're not better; *your* eyes haven't changed back. Not like mine have. So, why?"

Mani carried on looking vacantly at Leo's face. She was thinking, but not about that. She needed to go back to the cave now. She had the usual feeling that she had been away too long, that her father could appear at any minute. She had to go. She stood up.

"But, where are you going?" Leo stood still, his hands on his hips.

"I'm going to find my father," replied Mani matter-of-factly. For her, nothing had changed.

"But, don't you see? You must stay." Leo moved towards Mani. "We need to talk. We need to work this out…scientifically."

Mani pulled away. She was tired now. She wanted to go. And Leo was worrying her with all this talk.

"At least eat before you go." Leo tried. "Noodles? We can get it ready now? Come on!"

Mani felt herself being ushered through the door and guided to a seat in the insect-belly room, while Leo hurried to make her noodles. He kept talking, glancing over every now and then to check she wasn't trying to leave.

"I'm better, Mani. And I think it was you. You cured me. Somehow, you pulled the disease from me. I think,

59

Mani…you have something. There's something special about you…your blood…Do you understand?"

Mani switched the torch on and off. On—*click*—and—*click*—off. This would be useful. She could use it in the cave.

"And see—the electricity—it doesn't harm you!" Leo stopped and looked at Mani. "And we saw it—do you remember? Under the microscope? Your blood was different from mine—but I didn't know what it meant? But now…".

Leo pushed a bowl of steaming noodles in front of Mani. Her stomach grabbed at the warm savoury smell. She would eat this and then get back to the cave, as quickly as she could. Perhaps her father was back already? Whatever Leo was talking about could wait. For ever. But just one last meal…She set the torch down on the table and started to eat.

"This is a breakthrough. A scientific breakthrough. This changes everything," Leo carried on, sitting in front of Mani, staring at her intently. "Do you know what this is?" Leo pointed at an embroidered shape on the front of his white shirt.

Mani looked up as she shovelled the hot noodles into her mouth. Stitched in red on Leo's shirt pocket was a small symbol—it was a triangle inside an oval. The top of the triangle broke through the oval and the line across formed the letter "A". Mani had seen the same shape printed on lots of things inside the insect-building.

"This is who I work for. The Ark. I've worked for them all my life."

Mani looked at the torch. It had the same shape printed on it.

"Yes, that's right." Leo nodded vigorously. "Everything here is owned by the Ark. Have you heard of it? Do you know what they—we—do?"

Mani stared steadfastly at the torch. She would definitely take it with her, she decided.

"The Ark is an elite science organization. Its mission is to use science to save the world. My work for them is all I've ever cared about. It's all I know." Leo's eyes shone with pride. "I thought it was all over for me. I thought I was dying." He turned away from Mani then and looked around him. "But that's all changed now," he declared, placing his hand firmly on the table next to Mani. "You've changed that, Mani. *You* are the answer. You carry some kind of cure to the sickness, I'm sure of it. And the Ark can do something with you. With this." He gestured between them, as if their fates were somehow connected. "They have the skill, the money, but most of all, it's what we're all about. The Ark will save humanity from extinction!

"It's no good us staying here now," he continued. "I can't do anything on my own. I don't have the equipment—I don't even have phones or computers to tell anyone, since I cut all the electrics. There is nothing left here. But the Ark—if I can get you there—they will know what to do. They can develop it—whatever it is that you have—and then share it with everyone.

61

We can stop this evil disease, Mani." He paused. "You are the answer," he repeated. "You, Mani. You…" he trailed off.

Mani didn't know about all this. She didn't feel any different. A moment ago, she'd just been Mani—a girl who might be dying, the last child in her village. A girl who'd lost everything: her mother, her father, *her* world. And she still wanted them back—so what had changed, really? And yet this science-man was telling her that she could—she *had* to—save the rest of the world?

"Mani." Leo's voice was decisive. "I have to get you to the Ark. As soon as possible—so we have to leave tomorrow. On foot. There's no other way. To the Ark. We will make the journey together and I will look after you, will make sure you are safe. We will get there. Do you understand?"

Mani had had enough. She wasn't going anywhere. She was waiting for her father—hadn't she said that already? She pushed the empty bowl away from her and stood up. She shook her head.

"I will wait for my father," she said quietly. "I will not go. I will not go with you. I will not go with anyone. I will wait for my father."

She picked up the torch from the table and looked at its emblazoned *A*. It felt wrong taking it—it wasn't hers to take—but she wanted it and so she stowed it in her bag anyway.

And then she turned and left.

"So you wanna steal light, huh?" It was pitch black and the voice Mani could hear was snarky and nasal.

"Who are you? What do you want? Where's Ooshaka?"

"Ooshaka's on her way, kid," the voice replied.

Mani peered into the darkness but could see nothing—it was like someone had put a dark hood over her head.

"We thought this one was for me, if it's OK with you, ma'am?" The whiny voice cracked slightly with mock politeness.

Mani shivered. "Where's the snow? Where's the sunshine? And where's Ooshaka?" she repeated.

"Like I say," came the voice again, "you're after light—I get that. And you know what, kid? I admire your verve. You need to take charge." The voice lowered to a whisper. "Wanna see something cool?"

"But I can't see anything. It's too dark." This was annoying. She'd come to talk to Ooshaka, not to play some silly game.

"A-a-a-h," came the voice, although it sounded a bit like, *C-a-a-w*. "You can see a bit, if you try harder. Come closer, kid."

Mani lifted her arms to feel in front of her as she moved in the direction of the voice. In the blackness, her hands appeared dismembered, pulled apart from her body, like two white gloves dancing before her.

"That's it, that's it, kid. D'you see anything now?"

In front of her, the blackness began to float apart in a rich oily sheen. And there were overlapping lines and curves leading up to a head shape and a single bulbous black eye.

"Better, huh?" came the voice quietly.

Mani found she was looking at a crow.

"I've seen it all, kiddo. And light's one of the best. Let me show you." The bird jabbed his beak towards a cloth bundle, tied up by the corners in a neat knot. There was a rustling and rummaging of feathers being shaken. "Hop on board."

Mani found herself engulfed in the black oiliness of the crow's body. She hadn't noticed how large the bird was, but now she was sitting on its back with the cloth bundle squeezed between her knees.

There was a searing "R-a-a-a-a-wk" and two huge black wings exploded out. Mani held her breath and wrapped her arms around the bird's neck. There was movement beneath her—two leaps forward and the giant wings dragging powerfully down through the air and up, then down and up.

Mani held on tight. The crow was flying upwards, but in the darkness it was impossible to see. And, in any case, her eyes were screwed tightly shut and she could hear only the whooshing sound of the giant wingbeats, and the steady thunder beat of her own heart. If she let go, she would be thrown backwards, out into the darkness, and lost for ever.

After a while, the bird's body levelled out, and the wings stopped dragging. Mani opened her eyes. They

64

were moving smoothly—gliding—through the darkened world.

The crow called back to her, "Untie the bundle, kiddo, but don't look inside."

Mani shuffled the bundle up to her arms. Squeezing her legs round the bird's body to steady herself and holding on with one hand, she pulled the cloth ties open with the other.

The crow called again, "Now, hold on. Real tight, this time."

Then the bird dived sharply. Mani grabbed onto its neck with both arms, but lost hold of the bundle, which flew up. She managed to grab the edge of the fabric, but not in time to stop its contents flying everywhere.

"That's it! Perfect!" came the call, followed by a victorious, "C-a-a-a-w r-a-a-a-w-k!"

Mani could see, spilling out from the bundle, thousands—millions—of tiny lights, which now pinned themselves to the darkness, like bright jewels on a heavy curtain, illuminating everything. And in the centre was a luminous white sphere.

In the new light, the crow's feathers swam with opulent colour—blues and greens and purples—and Mani could see the filaments and texture in each one of the thick black feathers.

Mani stared into the moonlike ball. Her eyes ached in the glare. And, as she stared, she realized it wasn't the crow's light she was looking at. She was back in the cave, staring into the blinding beam of white light from the torch.

Chapter 12

Mani slept fitfully that night. She dreamed heavily of black curtains and sparkling jewels and talking crows. And she was following someone across an empty landscape—someone she wanted to see more than anything—but she could never catch up with them. They were always just a black shadow, just out of reach, and every time she got close enough to grab them, they disappeared.

She woke with her heart beating fast. But she found the world had been transformed. Instead of the murky darkness of the cave that she'd become used to, everything was drowning in a bright orange light. The sun had returned at last.

She blinked into the new light flooding through the cave entrance. She could see the owl had returned, as it did each morning, to rest. It was preening—plumping out downy white feathers from beneath the sleeker mottled brown ones on its wings, stroking its beak carefully along each one. It stopped and looked at Mani. *What are you waiting for?* it seemed to be saying. And Mani didn't know. Perhaps she wasn't waiting anymore.

The cave looked strange now—it was like she was seeing it for the first time. There were colours and textures she'd never noticed before. The sealskin which had been her bed all this time wasn't dark grey after all, but a pale white with light-grey dappled spots. And what had been a backdrop of impenetrable black at the back of the cave revealed itself to be endless clusters of chalky-white and pink stalagmites—turrets and minarets extending back as far as she could see, like a miniature city. Stacked beside her, next to the sealskin, were all the empty jars of food. There was nothing left. And at the front of the cave, pushed to the side, was the sled that she and her father had dragged here, loaded with all they owned, on the day they had left the village.

There was a sudden noise. Mani looked to see if the owl was on the move, but it remained motionless. The noise came again—a crumbling sound of rocks being dislodged and falling. Father? Tatka? Could it be? Had the sun brought him home at last?

Mani scrambled to the entrance of the cave and looked out—the rocks and the river were there as usual, but even they looked different. No longer moonlit and silver-grey, they were bathed in orange-yellow sunlight and appeared hot and red and dusty. The sun was a

68

full burning circle. She could feel its warmth seeping through her skin.

But, however hard she looked, she couldn't see anything moving in the landscape in front of her. She sat on a rock at the entrance to the cave, just below the owl's perch, and allowed her eyes to roam slowly across the rocks and along the twists and turns of the river. The owl stared out too, blinking its eyes slowly. Father was finally coming back. Mani breathed in long and slow. She knew it.

There was the sound again. A scuffing of shoes, and rocks cracking and cascading down.

Mani stood up now to see better. "Father? Tatka? Is that you?" she called out.

There was a muttering and cursing, and Leo's head appeared from behind a large boulder just in front of the cave entrance. He was sweating. His thin wispy hair stuck to his head in stripes, and his beard was ragged against his white shirt.

Mani slumped back down onto the rock. Her body and head felt heavy.

"Ah! Here you are!" beamed Leo. He craned his neck to see her and held his hand over his brow. He was panting heavily. "So, this is where you live!"

Mani couldn't bear to look at him. She had wanted so much for it to be her father.

Leo leaned on the rock, huffing and puffing and spluttering. "Listen." He gulped for air. "I've been thinking. Your father—he's not coming back. I think you know that?" He squinted up again at Mani.

She stared into the rock in front of her.

Leo carried on: "You've run out of food. I've nearly run out. We're running out of options here." He took a deep breath in and steadied himself.

Still, Mani didn't look up.

"So, I've been thinking…The best thing, I think, all round, now I'm better, and now we know…what we know—" he pointed towards Mani— "about you, is for us to go. Find your father…". He paused and looked up at Mani, stroking the end of his beard, searching for a reaction.

Mani looked up now and stared at him.

"I've got just about enough food to get us there. A couple of weeks, I reckon. We'll head to the Ark. We're bound to find your father on the way, and if not…it's the only place he could have gone to…There's nowhere else. See?"

He pulled a folded map out of his pocket and held it up. "And, if he was coming back, if he could, he would have…by now. Does that make sense?" He drew a line across the map with his finger. "See? Nothing between here and the Ark. Just flat plains and forest and mountain. If he hasn't come back here, the Ark is the only place he can be. And if we don't go now…well…we're going to die of starvation."

Mani looked out of the cave, still scanning the land for signs of her father. She looked back inside the cave. She saw the chalk marks she'd made on the wall, counting the days her father had been away. Thirty-five.

"I think we can find your father—I think he's out there," continued Leo, "and you stand more chance of finding him if you go to look for him rather than staying here. Do you understand, Mani?" He paused, and then continued in a loud staccato voice, "If we stay here, we die. We will go to find your father. We'll go to the Ark."

Mani took a deep breath in, and finally she nodded slowly. Yes, she understood. The food had run out. Her stomach told that story daily. And her father hadn't come back. But did this mean he wasn't going to come back? Ever?

She looked Leo straight in the eyes. "Yes, I understand," she said finally.

"Excellent. Well. Tell you what." Leo climbed up, now, onto the large rock right in front of Mani, and peered inside the cave. "Not sure what you want to bring, but I'll need to sort a few things. Let's meet tomorrow morning, at the river beach, just down there. We'll meet at sunrise." He pointed at the sun. "Kind of now-ish? But tomorrow. And take it from there."

Mani sat at the gaping hole of the cave entrance that proclaimed her father's ongoing absence.

Leo seemed about to say something else, but then thought better of it. He turned and started to make his way down the rock.

"Right-o," he muttered. "Bring what you need! But travel light. It's a bit of a stroll we've got ahead!"

71

Chapter 13

Father is not coming back. It was hard to accept. However many times Mani said these words, she couldn't get the idea to stick. And saying the words out loud just threw up more questions. If he wasn't coming back, where was he? Had something happened to him? Or had he decided not to come back? And if so, why?

Mani was squatting on the rock at the entrance to the cave, crushing chalk stone into the ground. She had a bigger, harder grey rock in her hand, and she was using it to grind the soft white stone. The chalk, which her father had given her to mark the passing days on the cave wall, was being transformed into a small pile of white powder.

Mani was tired and her thoughts had become jumbled. She hadn't slept, but she hadn't tried to. She was afraid that, if she slept and her father did return, she might miss him and lose him for ever. She willed with all her body and soul for him to appear. The harder she tried to imagine him there, the harder she pummelled the chalk into the ground, and the finer the white powder became. But she had to try. Because, if he came back now, things would be a whole lot simpler. They could stay here and carry on from where they'd left off. And she wouldn't have to go anywhere. But then she had to stop thinking—because that thought opened up a whole new world of uncertainty. Where had they left off? This wasn't their home. And her mother was still dead. How could they carry on?

Before her father had left, they had had one last conversation, sitting side by side at the entrance to the cave, where Mani sat now. But the conversation hadn't been good.

"Why can't I come with you, Tatka?" Mani had asked, holding desperately onto her father's sleeve.

"It's not safe," her father had replied simply. "And I don't know what I'll find. The world has changed."

They'd sat in silence. This wasn't unusual. Her mother would have filled in the gaps with talk and comforting hugs—but, since she'd gone, Mani and her father had simply allowed the huge silences to exist between them, like yawning valleys between mountainsides.

"I've come with you before." Mani tried again, looking at her father sideways.

Her father had shaken his head and carried on staring forward—his jaw set and his wolfish eyes fixed on the horizon. "It's different now. And I'll be quicker if I go alone—I'll take the boat out, I'll catch us some fish and go up to the trading post. It's four days there and four days back at the most. You'll be fine. And we need more food." His voice was brittle, as if he was fighting something else that he really wanted to say.

They'd watched the sun go down together. But, now Mani thought about it, she realized she couldn't recall what her father's eyes had been like that day. His eyes were distinctive—a craggy grey colour, and one eye had an amber line in it which seemed to weep from the pupil, down across the grey iris, to the white. But Mani couldn't remember noticing her father's eyes as they had talked. Was it because they hadn't really looked at each other? Did her father have the sickness too? Had his eyes been normal, or had they changed? Surely she'd remember that? But everything was mixing up now—Leo's eyes, her eyes, her mother's eyes. Perhaps her father was ill? Perhaps he had the sickness? Perhaps he was dying. But Mani could save him, if Leo was right about it all, if only he would come back.

They had sat in silence and darkness had descended. "*Morka* is here," her father had said. "*Morka*—our friend, the darkness of the polar night. It's the best time for me to go. It will be safer."

Mani had shivered.

"Don't fear the dark, Mani," her father had said. "At least we can still be sure of some things—our world might have changed, but our sun and moon just carry on. And so should we. Let the darkness be—allow it to embrace you, do not fight it—and, as sure as the sun will return and *morka* will retreat, so will I return to you."

He'd pushed a small leather pouch containing the small pieces of chalk stone into Mani's hand. He'd taken one out and drawn a thick short line down the wall.

"Use these to make a mark each day. This is how you'll know how many days have gone by. And you'll know, when you reach eight, I'll be back soon." He'd pointed to the jars inside the cave. "Each time you make the mark, remember to eat. Just once a day. We need to make it last. And I will return with more food. I promise."

Mani looked at all the chalk lines she'd marked on the wall. She felt a flush of anger and a burning in her cheeks, and she pressed harder with her grey rock, claiming the last fragments of chalk that hadn't been crushed. There was a decent amount of powder now, and she stepped down from the rock to reach into the water at the base of the cave. She dripped water into the chalk powder and mixed it to make a paste.

There was a pinkish glow on the horizon. Mani was nearly out of time. As soon as the sun pushed properly over the edge, that was it—no more waiting. She would have to go and meet Leo as they had arranged.

Come on, Tatka, she willed, stirring the chalky mixture with her fingertips. Come on.

But the entrance to the cave remained empty.

Mani dipped her whole hand into the chalk mixture now, covering her palm and each of her fingers and thumb in the white paste. Then she went to the bit of wall where she'd been marking the days off and pressed her hand against it. When she pulled it away, a white handprint was left. She hoped her father would understand. She hoped he would know that this was her leaving.

Then she dipped her finger into the chalky mixture and started to smear a shape on the wall. A squashed circle first, and then a triangle which intersected it to form the English letter *A*. Her father would know. This was where she had headed. The Ark. And if—*if*—her father ever made it back here, and *if* Mani had been wrong to go, her father would find these signs and he could follow her there.

The edge of the sun was visible over the horizon now and rising quickly. There was no more time. Leo would be on his way. Mani wiped her hand on the floor of the cave, checked her whalebone-handled knife was in the holster, and picked up her caribou-skin bag with the torch and the mask inside. She slung it over her shoulder and across her chest, and then pushed the sled to the cave entrance. They could use this to carry whatever Leo was bringing, for some of the journey at least.

Dragging the sled down the rocks, Mani left the cave without looking back. She was on her way. She was going to meet Leo. Together, they were going to find her father.

And they were headed to the Ark.

"What did they tell you about the ice, Mani?"

Mani was sitting next to Ooshaka at the edge of an ice cliff. Her legs dangled in the empty air, but the ice beneath her bottom felt strong and cold. Ahead was the open sea. Mani could see giant icebergs floating. Some were small—the size of boats—but others were colossal and seemed to Mani to be as big as whole planets.

"What do you mean, Ooshaka? What did who tell me?" Mani looked sideways at the polar bear's long white snout and black eyes, which were narrowed in thought.

"I mean, what do you know about that time, all those years ago, when the ice covered the Arctic? What did they tell you?"

Mani remembered sitting beside her mother, listening as her voice guided her through the ice world, telling her about her grandparents, and great-grandparents, and great-great-grandparents, and how they had lived. That was how she knew about the ice.

"Matka—my mother—she told me stories," she said eventually. "She was good at that. And they were always about the ice time. Like it is here. About our ancestors."

Ooshaka nodded.

Mani could hear her mother's excited voice in her head as she recounted tales of long treacherous journeys across the ice, and encounters with strange animals and spirits of the sea and sky.

"She thought the ice time sounded good," she continued. "Because everyone knew where they were. It held things in place. And you could go out hunting, across the frozen sea, and get further, and find more. The ice kept everyone safe." She pressed her hand into the icy ground next to her and watched the tiny ice particles stick to her fingers.

Ooshaka put her giant paw beside Mani's hand. "What else?" the polar bear asked.

"There were seasons—each year was the same: ice time, followed by ice break-up time, ice time, break-up time. You could count on the ice to tell you what time of year it was."

Ooshaka shuffled on the snow next to Mani to get more comfortable. She lay down and rested her snout on her two front paws. "This is good, Mani. I like this. Tell me more."

"Well, when it all melted, everything got all muddy and murky and confused. Places flooded, so people had to move. And it got hotter. And we couldn't grow things because the soil got too wet. People got hungry. Matka said we were lucky that our village was so far away from all the trouble. And she said that even though we can't bring the ice back, we can talk about it, and that sort of keeps it alive."

Ooshaka nodded approvingly. Then she turned sharply to look at Mani. "I bet she never told you that the ice sings."

Mani felt herself being scooped and pushed forward by Ooshaka's front paw. Suddenly, she was falling—over the edge of the ice cliff and downwards through streams of icy air, until she landed on the iceberg below. Ooshaka was beside her.

Apart from the sound of water gently churning at the edge of the iceberg, all was quiet. Then Ooshaka whispered, "Listen."

And, as they sat side by side on the iceberg, Mani could hear a strange sound. A creaking, grinding, wistful moan. Keeping still, she whispered, "I can hear it. Is it singing? Or talking? I can't tell whether it's sad or happy."

Ooshaka nodded. "Perhaps the iceberg is saying it doesn't matter. It is both. That sound is all these lumps of ice bumping into each other. They're all moving, all the time. Moving on. Staying and leaving. Changing places. Happy and sad."

There was a huge wrenching sound as the ice on which they were sitting broke free and started to drift slowly through the water. Mani looked around her. They were floating in the middle of the sea. As they passed other icebergs, she could hear the sounds of the iceberg conversations as they held and released each other.

"Moving on and staying. Happy and sad," Ooshaka was saying in a low bass voice that rumbled on and on, deep below the iceberg's haunting melodies.

Chapter 14

"Of course, this all used to be ice!" Leo was tramping ahead and called back to Mani. The sled was attached to a harness round his waist and his body tipped forward as he heaved it through the boggy sand.

They had loaded all that they could carry onto the sled—mostly Leo's remaining food supplies, but also a rucksack containing a tent and sleeping bags, a small gas ring to boil water, two tin cups, two bowls, and some matches. Leo had then attached a triangular flag on a thin baton to the back of the sled, on which was emblazoned the squashed circle and *A* symbol of the Ark. "To help keep us safe," he had said knowingly, adjusting the flag so it stood higher and bristled in the breeze.

Leo had also shown Mani a map of the journey they would take. The first bit followed the river towards the sea, before cutting inland to head through the forest to the mountains, and up to the Ark. Leo had glanced sideways at Mani as he explained how he hoped they might come across her father along the way, or at least a clue as to where he might be. Then he had folded the map up and tucked it into his shirt pocket, and they had set off.

To start with, Leo went ahead, pulling the sled and all the provisions on the understanding that later they would take turns. For now, Mani trudged behind. As the cave and the research station got further away, she felt a strange sensation. She'd only ever been as far as "one sleep away" from the village, and by tomorrow they would be way beyond this. She felt like she was climbing a tall tree and someone was sawing at the bottom as she tried to get higher. It was a sharp feeling of immediate danger, a feeling that, at any moment, she could fall catastrophically to the hard ground. She kept walking. It was easier to focus on keeping her legs and feet moving under her, one step at a time. So this was what she did. One squelching foot after the other.

She could hear Leo calling back to her every now and then: "Of course, if it was ice, it would be a bit easier to walk, wouldn't it!"

From behind, Mani could see how each step that Leo took seemed to get sucked into the soggy ground, and how his shoes and the bottom of his trousers were splattered with the pale silty sand. The river had widened now, and it was as if the water had seeped into the land, turning everything soggy. Leo was trying to navigate a sensible path. Too close to the water and the sand became too wet and unstable to walk on, but too far inland it became tangled with dying plants and huge thirsty snake-like roots and thick black clouds of mosquitoes.

The sun was rising in the sky and it was getting hotter. Mani wasn't thinking about anything, other than her aching feet. The trainers that Leo had given her, and had insisted she wore to undertake the journey, were too big and rubbed. She wanted to take them off and walk barefoot, like she had become used to, but that would mean getting Leo to stop and wait, and Leo seemed to want to get on. Mani kept up with the sled, grumbling inwardly about how much her feet hurt. With each passing minute, the sun got higher, and the air hotter.

"Ice as far as you could see!" Leo was still talking, half to himself and half to Mani. "Can you imagine? What a sight that would have been! What a world, eh?"

Mani kept her eyes fixed on the sand ahead and concentrated on moving forward.

Leo stopped for a moment and looked around. The sled came to a standstill, and the rope that was attached to his waist coiled loosely on the ground. "What a loss!" He shook his head and wiped his shirt sleeve across his forehead. Then, under his breath, "What a mess."

Mani eyed the sled. Between the food supplies and the rucksack was a small gap. A place for someone to *sit down*; she felt her legs buckle beneath her slightly.

Leo was muttering to himself, his back to Mani, and, although the thought only lasted a split second, it was time enough for Mani to decide; she stepped lightly onto the sled, wiggled her bottom in between the bags, and sat down. It felt better. Just lifting her feet out of the heavy sand for a moment was a relief. Before she was even able to think about calling out to Leo, to tell him she was just having a rest, the sled started to move again.

"I swear the damn thing's getting heavier!" Leo grumbled to himself. But he didn't stop and turn round.

What else could Mani do but sit and enjoy the ride?

Chapter 15

It felt so good. The weight was off Mani's throbbing feet. She pulled her shoes off and inspected the raw circles of red on her heels. Then she peered into the bags either side of her. They were crammed full of strange packets slapped with plain white labels that said, *freeze-dried food*. Mani pulled a few out and read the smaller print slowly and out loud. *Chick-en roa-st din-ner. Spag-het-ti car-bon-ar-a. Neo-po-li-tan ice-cream sand-wich.* These sounded good, whatever they were. But, as she marvelled at the thought of *peach-es and cre-am*, she became aware that the sled had come to a standstill.

"You are kidding me, right?" Leo was standing in front of her.

Mani stuffed the packets back in the bag and looked up. Trickles of sweat were dribbling down Leo's forehead. Mani couldn't see his eyes because his glasses were clouded with steam.

"We've got this long journey ahead...and you...you...and I'm—" He was so short of breath, he could hardly speak, and he pointed helplessly at Mani and the packed sled.

Mani stared back. She wanted to explain, but she didn't know what to say, or how to say it, and this seemed to exasperate Leo more.

He crouched down and steadied himself against the sled, until his breathing returned to normal. "This won't do...won't do at all...," he said quietly. He looked up and wagged his finger at Mani. "So don't give me that blank look."

Again Mani wanted to explain, but Leo moved on too quickly.

"Let's get one thing clear. You can get off that sled right now and walk and, when we stop, you'll take a turn pulling for a bit."

Mani got off the sled.

Leo was standing with his hands on his hips. "This won't work if we don't help each other. Do you understand?" He turned and marched to the front of the sled. The rope became taut again, and they moved off.

Leo was walking faster now, and the widening space between them was a relief. It was easier away from the wagging finger and vexed face.

Before long, Mani heard Leo's voice again, but now he was shouting: "Mani, Mani! Stop! Don't come any closer!"

Ahead, Leo was up to his knees in thick wet sand, his arms flailing and hands splashing as he tried to stop himself sinking. The sled beside him was half submerged. He reached out to the edge of the sled and pressed down on it to try to release his legs, but this only seemed to make things worse. The sled was sinking fast now, and Leo was up to his waist.

"Mani!" he shouted again. "It's quicksand! Stay where you are!"

But Mani knew about quicksand. Her father had taught her. She called out to Leo: "Still! Keep still!"

Leo stopped moving and looked at Mani. And he stopped sinking. The sled was almost gone, and Leo was still stuck up to his waist—but he wasn't going any deeper.

"Wait!" Mani called again. "Don't move!" She ran off and found a long, thick piece of root, then dragged it back, as close as she could to where Leo was stuck. "Lean . . . like this," she said, holding up the root in front of her vertically and letting it fall forward until it was horizontal.

Leo watched. "Yes, of course," he muttered. "I need to make my surface area bigger and displace the quicksand." He started to lean forward, and as he did so his legs and feet began to rise slowly but surely behind him.

Mani extended the piece of root out to him and, when he grabbed it, pulled it gently until Leo could crawl slowly to firmer ground. Once he was free, they both scrambled away from the treacherous quicksand to the tangled foliage, away from the water.

Leo was caked head to toe in mud, his trousers, shirt, face, and glasses completely painted in the fine pale sand, and, in the heat, it was beginning to bake and crack. Mosquitoes were swarming around him, but he didn't seem to notice. He looked back at the quicksand, where just the top of the Ark flag on the sled was still visible, and watched as it finally disappeared, engulfed by the greedy swamp.

Leo let his head fall into his hands. "We've lost everything." He looked up at Mani. "But we can't go back...we have nothing left."

Mani laid her hand protectively on her bag. This wasn't true. She still had all that she owned in the world—the torch and her mask—and she still had her knife. She hadn't lost anything. This wouldn't stop them: she would find a way—because she was going to find her father. And nothing could get in the way of that.

Chapter 16

They sat side by side, watching the thick circular ripples that radiated out across the boggy sand, all that was left now of the sled and their provisions. Mani stared into the ground. Beside her, Leo seemed crumpled, beaten. His head was hanging low. And, for that moment, Mani felt strangely tall next to him.

Beneath the brown and green tangled carpet of roots and stems, Mani could see an earthworm sidewinding its way across the sludge. Carefully, she threaded her fingers through the roots and plucked it out. She held it up. It was pink and plump. She looked over at Leo, who was still staring mournfully through mud-caked glasses at the quicksand.

"It's OK. We can find food to eat," Mani said, dangling the worm in the air between them. "Father taught me. There's plenty on the land—and in the sea. You just need to know where to look." And she dropped the worm into her mouth and chewed. It tasted nutty and mushroomy at the same time. Mani scoured the ground again and pulled another worm from the vegetation. "Here," she said, holding it out for Leo to take.

Leo stared at the writhing pinky-brown beast squeezed between Mani's thumb and forefinger, a grimace forming on his face. He didn't take the worm, so Mani shrugged her shoulders and tipped her head back and dropped it into her mouth and chewed.

"If you don't eat," she said, as she pulled another worm from the ground, "you will starve." She shuffled closer to Leo and held the worm in front of his face. It curled upwards between her finger and thumb. "They taste OK," she said. And she pushed it closer to him.

Finally, Leo took it. He peered over his glasses at it. He glanced back at Mani, and then, sticking his tongue out as far as he could, he placed the worm at the back of his mouth and, in one gulp, swallowed it without chewing. Mani thought he might be sick, but eventually he looked up and half smiled.

"OK, then." He sighed and took the map out of his shirt pocket. Wiping the mud from it, he spread it out on the ground in front of them and ran his finger up the stretch of river they had been following. "By my reckoning, we need to start heading inland soon and cross these plains." He looked ahead. "Over the brow of that hill, the landscape should open up and we'll be able

89

to see the forest. With a bit of effort, we can reach it by nightfall and camp there."

Mani nodded. She stood up. "We will look for berries on the way," she offered.

Leo smiled and stood up too. "Well, then, no time like the present!"

They set off, walking side by side. The air was hot and they had to constantly fling their arms around their heads to fend off the thick clouds of mosquitoes. But the half-rotten vegetation created a springy carpet to walk on, and without the weight of the sled they could walk much quicker. Their steps fell in time and a quiet harmony wrapped around them.

After a while, Leo stopped. Their path seemed to be bringing them closer to the sea. He took the map out of his pocket and stared over the grey water. A heavy haze hung in the air. Mani looked out to where Leo was squinting. The forest was visible in the distance across the water. But there were no open plains connecting them.

"You know what's happened?" said Leo eventually, waving the map impatiently. "This map is old. The water has risen. The plains are submerged. And we have been cut off. There's no way over there, other than by crossing the water." He shook his head and stared down at the map.

Mani carried on looking out at the sea. The more she looked, the more she realized that the water, as far as she could see, was riddled with filth and rubbish. What had looked like rocks and seaweed, and shells and pebbles, was in fact rubbish—millions of washed-up plastic bottles, laced with old plastic wrappers, strangulating coloured plastic rope and tangled fishing nets. And what had looked like flashes of silver fish darting in the shallow surf were in fact thousands of dead fish floating at the surface and washing up in a brown-tinged foam with the tide.

They stepped now towards the water, looking out at the forest beyond and the sea that separated them from it. The filthy sea churned and swirled dangerously, creating a foul-smelling teeming soup.

Leo turned to Mani. "And I can't swim," he said matter-of-factly.

Chapter 17

They wouldn't need to swim. They just needed a boat of some kind. And, if there wasn't a boat to hand, well, they would make one. And Mani knew how.

"We'll float across," she said. She picked up a blue plastic bottle and held it out to Leo.

Leo's face brightened. "Of course! Plastic bottles! The perfect flotation device." He began to shuffle along the shoreline, gathering bottles in his arms.

"But we'll need ones with lids," said Mani, discarding the one she was holding, "or it won't work!"

Leo nodded, releasing the armful of bottles he was holding to the ground. He scanned around. "This is going to be harder than I thought . . ." he muttered. "But not impossible!" He strode across the rubbish-strewn ground and picked up a large plastic bottle. He held it up in the air triumphantly. "With a lid!"

"And look here!" Mani called to him. She was holding a large plank of sea-smoothed wood in one hand and a coil of blue plastic rope in the other. "We can make a raft."

Together, they set about gathering up anything that looked useful and piled it up at the water's edge. It was hot work, and the sickening smell was almost unbearable. Every now and then, Mani paused and raised her face to the wind that was picking up, to try to draw some clean air into her lungs.

After a while, Leo started to arrange what they had found into some sort of order. Mani began working with the fragments of rope, splicing and tying—just as her father had shown her. Leo began tying pieces of wood and plastic together. They worked silently. Mani ventured further along the shoreline to find more bottles and longer pieces of rope. Each time she returned with more, Leo grunted a sort of thank you. "It's simply a matter of making ourselves less dense than the fluid we will sit on…," he muttered to himself.

A raft slowly took shape—two planks of wood, with rows and rows of neatly tied plastic bottles beneath.

"Let's try it out," said Leo, dragging the craft into the shallow slap of surf and dead fish. Mani sat at the water's edge and took her trainers off. She stowed them in her bag and splashed through the water to climb on.

The raft bobbed happily enough with Mani on board, but as soon as Leo tried to get on too, it tilted, and waves toppled over it and started to drag it down.

"We need more bottles," Mani said, as Leo struggled to clamber out of the shallow water, shaking his head.

"Agreed," he muttered. "The ratio is all wrong."

Then something caught Mani's eye. Beside them at the shoreline were what looked like two grey rocks. But they weren't rocks. They were covered in dappled spots and silky light-grey skin. And Mani could see big oily eyes and ragged whiskers. No, they weren't rocks at all, but the huge and bloated bodies of dead seals. Mani leaped off the raft.

They could use these. Her father would have taken out the bladders, and inflated them to use as floats, as the rest of the carcass and skin could be used for boat building, but they could use these bodies as they were, pumped full of gas from their decaying flesh. Because they would float. Mani pulled them up by the tails. They stank and she had to hold her breath, and clouds of flies buzzed angrily as she dragged them towards the raft.

Leo buried his nose in his shirt sleeve and helped Mani pull the bodies to the back of the raft. They set about wrapping a long piece of rope around their necks and tails to attach them. "They certainly float," he said, winding the excess rope in a coil and setting it on the raft. Then he climbed on board and looked with a satisfied smile at Mani.

A cold wind whipped across the landscape and some stray plastic bottles rattled and rolled along the shore before coming to a stop in the shallow water. Mani looked up at the sky. Dark clouds were gathering, and the surface of the water was spiking silver blades. A roll of thunder rumbled behind them.

Leo shivered. "The weather's turning. Perhaps we should wait till the storm passes."

Mani looked around. There was no shelter here, and who knew how long the bad weather would last? Just across the water, she could see the forest where they planned to camp. "But, if we go now," she said, "we might beat it." She jumped on board the raft in front of Leo. She had picked up the lids of two plastic boxes, and now she used these as paddles, scooping the water back to get the raft moving forward.

When they were out just a few metres, Mani turned to Leo. He looked terrified.

"I told you I can't swim, didn't I?" he said.

Mani began to answer, but her words were whipped away by the sound of crashing thunder and slapping waves. She turned and paddled furiously ahead as the first spits of rain jabbed and poked at her face.

Chapter 18

As the storm gained force, Mani clung onto the raft. All she could see ahead were the rising hammers of waves and, above, the huge anvils of metal-grey storm clouds. Her eyelids were being blown inside-out by the violent wind, and her clothes and skin were soaked shiver-cold from the pouring rain and the flaying ocean. She could no longer see the shore they had set off from, so turning back wasn't an option.

She had given up trying to paddle. The storm was throwing the raft almost vertical and she needed to use both arms to hold on. She was lying on her stomach and grasping the ends of the ropes they had used to secure the bottles. The excess rope flailed out into the ripping waves like tentacles. The muscles in her arms were burning and her fingers were numb.

She strained her head round to see Leo. But Leo had gone! She looked about frantically and saw, just behind the raft, in the heaving and churning water, Leo's head surfacing and gasping for air.

She hooked a leg under a secure stretch of rope and felt in her bag for her knife, holding it by the handle in her mouth. Then she reached out towards one of the seals and tied it to her wrist with a section of excess rope. She took the knife and cut the seal free of the raft, watching as its body was thrown back by the wind and water in the direction of Leo, and bracing for the pull against her wrist.

"Catch it!" she yelled into the marauding wind, unable to see if such a feat was even possible. She resumed her grip on the raft, keeping her eyes shut now as the storm continued its rampage. There was nothing else she could do but hope she had done enough to save Leo.

It felt like hours. Mani's arms were aching and her fingers burning from gripping so tightly. But eventually, almost as suddenly as it had started, the storm loosened. It was as if the heavens, bored with the game, were drawing in a breath and exhaling slowly rather than blusteringly as before. Dark clouds reluctantly gave way to light wisps and the waves slowly softened. Cautious pale-yellow beams of sunlight pushed from behind the retreating thunder clouds.

Mani finally relaxed her hands and arms, and she sat up, blinking through salt-soaked lashes. She felt as if she had been beaten up. Her body and head were stinging and throbbing from the assault by the wind and rain and waves.

Now, as if nothing had ever happened, the calm sea held her gently on the raft, like a cradle. She looked behind her. There, in the water, bedraggled (but somehow still wearing his glasses) and hugging the dead seal in a bizarre embrace, was Leo.

"I told you I couldn't swim!" he spluttered hoarsely. "And this thing stinks."

Mani smiled. She started pulling on the rope, which was still wound round her wrist, to bring Leo in closer to the raft.

"I can't get back on," Leo called from the water. "It sank, remember? When I got on? Before we used these beasts?" He slapped the dead seal on the side.

Mani stopped. Leo was right. The two of them together would be too heavy now, without both dead seals to add buoyancy. She looked towards the shoreline. It was within sight now and she could see rows of brightly coloured houses, which hadn't been visible before, and the line of forest behind them, which promised shelter for that night.

"I'll pull you, then," she said. "Just keep holding on." And she lay down on her tummy and used the last of her strength to paddle with her hands and propel them towards the shore.

As they got closer, a gentle swell of tide started to draw them in, and Mani sat up. Progress was slow, but it was nice to sit in the calm water and feel the easy movement of the raft towards the land, and the warmth of the sun. She looked at the pretty coloured houses, which seemed friendly enough, like rainbow-coloured gift boxes.

But, as she looked, Mani thought she saw a shadow moving past the coloured fronts; it was quick and low, and looked like an animal, darkening the buildings fleetingly, and then it was gone. What was it? She strained to see as the tide drew them ever closer. It didn't reappear, but it left Mani with the nagging feeling that something was watching them. She blinked, tired now. Perhaps she had imagined it.

The tide finally nudged them into the shallows. Mani dipped her bare feet into the water, which was surprisingly warm, and let them sink into the prickly sand. She splashed onto the beach. Leo crawled behind her, kicking the dead seal away in disgust. They had made it. They were alive. So why did Mani now feel so uneasy?

Chapter 19

"You did well out there," Leo said quietly, looking over the now-calm sea. "You kept me afloat . . . You saved my life."

The sun was beginning to lower in the sky.

"We'd better work out where we're going to sleep," he said, glancing at the row of houses behind them. "I wonder what all this is, here."

Mani felt overwhelmed by the need to sleep *right now*. Her limbs were heavy underneath her wet clothes and her eyelids were forcing themselves shut. She just wanted to curl up and close her eyes. She didn't know what the night ahead held and that was worrying. She squeezed her fists. Even the familiarity of the hard floor in the cave would have been welcome now.

But no. She was here. A quicksand bog, a channel of polluted water, and a violent storm now separated her from her old life. She was wet through. She was exhausted. And she was hungry again.

As they walked towards the row of colourful houses, Mani imagined cosy interiors, and the smell of cooking, and plump beds where they might sleep. She breathed in deeply, as if that might push away the feelings of worry, but, as she inhaled, she became aware of a vile stench. It was sickening. She covered her nose with her hand.

And now, as she looked at the houses properly, she could see it wasn't a pretty row of seafront cottages after all, but the ruins of buildings that had been destroyed by something violent. The windowpanes were all smashed, roofs were caving in, and through the gaping windows and wrenched-off doors she could see that inside they were full of water. Strange creeping snake-like water-plants had taken hold and were wrapping round and out and over the buildings, claiming them as their own.

"Looks like the water has risen here too," said Leo. "Probably comes and goes with the tide … Severe flooding, I should say." He peered through a window and grimaced. "We'd better make a move before it comes back in."

They walked past the houses, and Mani could see strange-looking objects floating on the trapped flood water—a doll lying corpse-like, an open suitcase, a mangled guitar, a shredded book—remnants of lives interrupted. Some objects had been washed outside too, and they had to step over a random selection of cutlery and clothes, chairs and cushions, and burned-out electrical equipment. It was as if the very buildings themselves were sick and spewing out their insides.

Leo shook his head. "We definitely can't stay here. We need to get to that forest as soon as possible...before it gets dark. We'll be safer there." He paused at the end house in the row and pulled the soaking map from his pocket, spreading it on the ground. "Let's hope this dries out—it's all we've got."

Mani peered into the house. Not only had the front door been ripped off, but the whole of the front wall was falling down. Through the opening, she could see a wonky dining table, set with a tablecloth and plates and glasses that had all tipped over. Up-ended chairs floated half-submerged in the water around the table, along with an array of saucepans and a kettle.

She kept walking, her hand held all the time to her face to mask the smell, which was getting stronger.

"Hold on a minute!" said Leo, putting away the map and standing up. "We could probably use some of this." He climbed over the collapsed wall into the house and waded to the table. He pulled at the tablecloth, allowing the glasses and plates to fall into the water, and folded it under his arm. Then he fished a saucepan out of the water.

"Oilcloth," he said to Mani as he climbed back out of the house. "Waterproof. We can lie on it." Then he waved the pan in the air. "And we can boil water in this, to drink."

Mani could hardly bear the smell now. It was sickening. She wanted to get away—and fast. But did she really want to go to the forest? Who knew what was there? What she really wanted was to run away from all of this—back home. She moved her hands to cover her eyes now, as well as her nose.

Leo looked at her. "Hey, we're going to be OK." he said, stepping forward as if he might reach out and touch her, but then thinking better of it. "Remember, we're going to find your father. And all this…is so we can get to a safe place. The Ark is the best possible place we could be." He adjusted the items he'd collected in his arms. "It's a good plan! We're going to be fine."

They carried on walking. Behind the houses, the true source of the smell became apparent. They were now crossing a bare expanse of soil, totally devoid of life; it looked like everything had been washed away by the flood water. But Mani could see stick-like objects poking out of the ground. And the further they got, the clearer it became what they were. Bones.

"It's some kind of graveyard," muttered Leo. "And the flood water has washed away the surface soil. So the bones are…at the surface. That explains the smell."

Mani started to run.

"Hey, hold on!" Leo called behind her.

But she couldn't bear it any longer. As she ran over the flood-washed soil towards the forest, all she could see were skeletal hands and bony fingers grasping at the surface, as if they were trying to clamber out. And black-eyed skulls grinned fiendishly at her, ribcages fanned across the ground as if gasping for clean air. Everything looked like it was trying to escape from something terrible. And, as if this

103

scene wasn't repulsive enough, there was something even more vile about the bones themselves: they were a strange red colour—just like the body Mani had seen in the boat by the cave. All the skeletal remains seemed to be pulsing with a peculiar red light, as if from within. And Mani knew now the choking smell was not only one of rotten flesh and decay, but was also tinged with an acrid smell of burning.

She kept running until she came to the edge of the forest, where she waited for Leo to catch up with her. They stopped, heaving for breath.

"The sickness," Leo said eventually. "They must have all…like us…but…God, it's awful…There are no survivors here." He looked back towards the houses, and then at Mani.

She shuffled uncomfortably under the intensity of Leo's gaze. He was staring deep into her eyes. Mani could see her own reflection in his dirty glasses, and there was the reminder. *She* hadn't escaped the disease. *Her* eyes were still buzzing with lines of electricity. She blinked slowly, as if this might switch it all off.

"It's quite peculiar," Leo said, after a pause, "that you should have this quality…this power, you might say…but just think of what we can do with it…if we get it to the right people…We could have saved these poor souls…We—you—could save everyone, Mani. It's hope…hope, when we thought everything was over."

Buoyed by that thought, Leo led the way now into the forest.

"Come on, let's find somewhere to camp."

Chapter 20

The sun was sinking fast now and, as they entered the forest, the tightly packed trees extinguished its final rays. In the dying light, it soon became clear there was nothing growing here. The forest was dead. The branches on the trees were bare and the floor was covered in decaying vegetation. The tangled roots and old dangling creepers created a sense of chaos and confusion. The air was warm and smelled musty, and Mani could feel it sticking in her nose and at the back of her throat. Every now and then, she felt her trainers squelch into stagnant pools in the sodden forest floor, the moisture evaporating into the air in a pungent mist.

They came to a sort of clearing where several trees had fallen. Leo sat heavily on one of the trunks. "We need to stop. There's no light left. This looks like as good a place as any. We can have a go at boiling some drinking water." He pointed to a brown pool of water that seemed to be crawling and bubbling with small beast life. He took the oilcloth from under his arm and spread it out on the soggy ground. "Better than nothing, eh?"

Mani looked around her. There it was again. A movement. The same as she'd seen on the shoreline. A darkening. An animal shadow, but only visible for a moment. And then gone. What was it? She looked over at Leo, who seemed oblivious to it.

"How do we go about lighting a fire, then?" Leo asked, standing up.

Mani began picking moss from the floor of the forest and the fallen trees. Her father had taught her this. It was a good way of getting a fire going, and right now she was glad of something to do—it stopped her thinking about the darkness. And that there was no dinner. And no bed to sleep in that night.

But the moss was as wet as everything else—she could wring water out of it. "We'll never light this," she exploded. "It's too wet." And she slumped down onto the log, her fists still squeezing the clods of soaking moss.

Leo was suddenly by her side. He looked at the moss, and then at Mani. "Hey, hey, hey," he soothed, although his voice was tinged with impatience. "Yes, I see what you mean…it is too wet."

Mani threw the moss to the ground and folded her arms across her chest.

"Right," said Leo. "Tomorrow. Top priority. Food and water. We will find some. And I will not rest until we have. OK?"

But that didn't help. Mani was feeling alone and small and hungry *right now*. She did what she had been wanting to do since she had left the cave. She felt in her bag for her mother's mask and pulled it out.

Leo sat down beside her. "What's that?" he asked. "I thought we were travelling light?" He grinned.

Mani held the mask carefully in her hands, fanning the feathers out where they had got wet. Leo leaned in to get a closer look. Mani didn't know where to start. "It's a mask. It was given to me. My mother was looking after it until I was old enough to have it," she said after a while.

Leo reached out his hand to touch the mask, but Mani pulled it back. The mask's empty eyes and inscrutable face looked back at them. Leo smiled, withdrawing his hand. "A birthday present?" he asked. "A toy? I shouldn't think you need to be a grown-up for that," he added with a dismissive wave of his hand. "She probably just didn't want it to get broken."

It wasn't a toy. Mani knew that. But how could she start to explain what it was—without sounding ridiculous? How could she put into words all that she had learned since she first put it on? "When I wear it," she said, "I get to go somewhere else. Another world. A world apart from this world." She gestured around her.

Leo sat up straight, now, and brushed his hands down his muddy trousers. "Ah! Well...I'm afraid I'm not the sort of person to play those kinds of make-believe games." He spoke in a sure, business-like voice, as if he'd uncovered some sort of truth.

Mani flinched. It wasn't make-believe. And it wasn't a toy. Leo didn't understand at all. And now she wanted to explain, because it was all she had, and so she tried again. "It's important. My mother is there. When I put it on. She's there—it's another place…a special world… I've been there…I've seen her already…She told me about it too, before she—"

Leo laughed and Mani felt her cheeks redden. He waved his hand now towards the mask, as if pushing it away. "You have a lovely imagination," he said, "but that won't work for a scientist, I'm afraid. But, go ahead, if it makes you feel better…"

Mani wished she had never even tried to talk to him about it.

When Leo spoke again, his voice was softer and kinder. "Mani, I'm sorry. You lost your mother. I do understand," he said. "I do know how it feels…I lost…" But he trailed off without finishing the sentence. "I had a daughter and she…well…that's for another time… but I get that you're missing her…and this isn't exactly ideal." He pointed around him at the forest. He stood up and started pulling the oilcloth straight. "But we have to make the best of what we've got."

He stopped and looked out into the distance, through all the trees, to somewhere else. "Because what we're doing now—this discovery, our gift to science—is very important." He looked at Mani again. "All I can say is…and you might not want to hear this…but, once they're gone, they're gone, and it's best for everyone if we keep going, keep busy, don't think about them too much; we need to get on with what we're here for. And, for me, well, that's to help the world out of this mess. And you? Well, you want to find your father… and then…well, who knows what you might be able to do?"

Mani didn't want to listen anymore. Leo was wrong. The mask was real. Hadn't she already met Ooshaka? And hadn't Ooshaka promised she would find her mother? How would Leo explain that? Was that just her imagination?

Mani turned her back on Leo. She heard him stand up and start picking through leaves and twigs on the forest floor. She let her focus settle on the mask. It started to glow. She watched the light gently pulsing in her hands, and the feathers peeling away in leaves of light. She lifted it and pulled the mask onto her head, placing her hands over her ears to shut Leo out. But, just as she pulled it down over her face, she saw it again—the animal shadow, slinking along the fallen trunk behind Leo. A dark shape, close now. Four crouching legs, a full sinuous tail, and ears pricked like soldiers on the watch. And as it moved Mani felt the air move and shimmer behind the mask and over her face. And it was there for just a moment, in front of her, and then it was gone.

109

"Where is she, Ooshaka? Where is she? I want to see her now. You promised. I'm fed up with waiting for answers." Mani was sitting between Ooshaka's front paws, her back leaning into the bear's chest and her fists clenched. Crow was sitting opposite on the flat ice. Behind, the sky was clear bright blue, and the sun yellow.

"You heard the kid," echoed Crow. "She wants her mama. And she wants her now. People are telling her she's gone! Tell her. Tell her the truth."

Ignoring Crow, Mani folded her arms across her chest and looked up at the underside of Ooshaka's chin, which was covered in the most exquisite soft hair. She pushed an elbow back and gently nudged Ooshaka in the chest.

"What's the point in coming here?" she demanded. "If you can't bring me to her?"

"You heard her, Bear—what's the point in her coming here?" Crow echoed.

Crow was annoying. Mani didn't need his help. She wanted to talk to Ooshaka alone.

"Oh, be quiet," she snapped at Crow. "I'm here to talk to Ooshaka."

Crow turned his head to the side to stare with one black oily eye at Mani. He winked.

"Yes, hop it, Crow," laughed Ooshaka. "I'm the one that's useful here…for now."

Crow looked up towards Ooshaka and let out a jeering "Cr-a-a-w-r-a-a-wk!" Then, "Suit yerselves, kiddos. But I'll be back. Old Crow has his uses too, you know! *Adios, amigos! Auf wiedersehen! Au revoir! Adieu!*" And, with a dramatic sweep of his rich black wings, he galloped one-two-three across the ice and flew away.

Mani watched his silhouette gradually get smaller and smaller against the bright sky, until it became just a black pinprick.

That was better. It was quiet. They could talk now. Mani leaned back into Ooshaka. The bear's body was soft and warm, and Mani felt her anger melting away.

Finally, Ooshaka spoke: "What will you do when you find her? You know she can't come back with you, right?"

Mani thought for a moment. Of course Matka couldn't come back with her. She was dead. She had to stay here. If she was here at all. And Mani was alive. She couldn't stay in this world.

She looked out across the ice. It was empty and white and featureless. It was nothing like the world they had lived together in. Nothing like their home. Their small house. Their noisy mealtimes—friends and neighbours popping in all the time. Their stories at bedtime. Their songs. What would it be like to stay with her in this empty ice world? What would they do? How could they fill their time? There would be no house, no home, nothing to do. Mani didn't say anything.

111

"OK," said Ooshaka. "How about this, then? How do you *want* it to be, when you find her?"

As she spoke, a gust of wind blew in, and with it came a blast of light icy snow. The gust was so strong, it blew Mani's hair back. But, as the beams of sun penetrated the ice droplets, a fracturing happened, and the pure white rays were broken into a rainbow that seemed to be all around them, each individual colour dancing and playing over the surface of the ice. And Mani could see it over her T-shirt and on the skin of her hands—all the different colours at once laying a vibrant patchwork over everything. She looked at Ooshaka and could see her fur too had been transformed into glorious colour.

And Mani knew then—this was how she wanted it to be. She could feel it, although she didn't have the words for it. It was all here at the same time. The yellow of laughter. The green of calm. The blue of sadness. The pink of joy. The orange of creativity. The purple of hope. The red of anger. And all the colours of love. All the things she'd shared with her mother. All the things that had gone when she had gone. And she wanted all of them back. All at once.

And finally she could answer Ooshaka. "I want it to be like this," she said quietly.

Chapter 21

"I told you we'd find something! Didn't I promise?"

Leo stood with outstretched arms and presented the scene that had just come into view as if he had created it himself.

Mani could see a small cottage in a clearing in the forest.

It was still early morning, but Mani felt like she had been squelching over the seething forest floor for hours. And the sameness had been relentless: endless, leafless trunks that constantly cheated them of a horizon, always dashing the hope that at any moment they might break through to the other side.

Mani was thirsty. She longed for clean water. She had wiped handfuls of dirty liquid from the puddles in the forest floor across her lips every now and then, but the water—if it was water—was full of moving bits and tasted revolting. Her lips were cracked, and her tongue was sticky in her mouth. The sight of the clearing and the cottage, and the promise of what might be inside, made her dizzy. She stumbled to a stop behind Leo.

"Is it real?" Even her voice was cracked.

"It is real indeed!" beamed Leo. "And it looks like someone is living here!" He strode towards the cottage. "Didn't I promise? Food and water? Didn't I say?" he called behind him.

The cottage was, in fact, more of a wooden hut. It was built over two floors and had small windows and a covered porch area on which there was a rocking chair draped with a quilted blanket and a cushion. Beside the front door, logs were neatly stacked. One of the upstairs windows was open and a floral curtain billowed out, which was strange, as the air was so still, but the homely scene called them forward nonetheless, inviting them in.

At the door, Leo raised his hand to knock, but the door opened itself. He peered inside. "Hello?" he called. "Anyone home?" He turned to Mani. "Looks like someone is still living here, but we'd better go in… see if they're…" He nodded to himself and took a deep breath, stepping inside and calling out every now and then, "Hello?" and, "Anyone here?"

Mani followed. Inside was a prettily furnished living room, with sofas, chairs, cushions, and rugs. But, after so long outside, it felt small, and when the door shut behind them, it was like a lid closing on a box. There was a cloying floral smell and Mani had a strong feeling that

114

what they were doing was wrong. But her mouth was dry and jagged. If she could just get some clean water—there was bound to be some here—then they could go.

Above her, Mani saw that the ceiling light had been pulled out. On the walls, plug points and switches had been pulled away, leaving frayed wiring that looked like headless snakes trying to escape. Electricity had been cut. It looked like the disease had been here.

Along the far wall was an open wooden staircase. After so long in the forest, Mani had an urge to go up them. She wanted to look through a window—to try and see at least where they were, and where they might be headed.

She climbed the stairs slowly. At the top, directly ahead, was a bathroom with a small window and a sink. She wrenched the taps on. There was a clanking and a gurgling and the whole house seemed to shudder. But then came the water. Beautiful clear cold water. At last.

Mani bent her head and started to drink, slurping and gulping as much as she could. Her stomach gurgled and ached with the onslaught. When she couldn't drink any more, she squeezed her eyes shut and splashed it over her face and into her hair. It felt cool. She rubbed her face, enjoying washing away the mud and grime.

She opened her eyes. Over the sink was a mirror. She stared. Her eyes were really quite something. She bent forward to see better. They were still flashing and flickering and strangely beautiful. The tiny hairline lightning strikes crackled brightly and endlessly in shades of pale purple and white and red. How was this all just carrying on—inside her—without her? She felt fine. She couldn't be sick. But Leo had said all this made her special. Perhaps she was.

"Mani! Mani!" Leo called from downstairs. "Come quick!"

Mani paused for a moment. She looked out of the window. At the back of the cottage was a neatly kept garden, planted hopefully with vegetables that were now dying. Withered plants clung to bamboo sticks and small knots of shrivelled vegetables sat in neat rows.

Then something caught her eye. To one side, there was what looked like a pile of old clothing. But, as Mani looked harder, she could see that the clothes were actually filled with something. Bodies—lying face down. There were three. The middle one was much smaller than the other two—a child—and its legs were twisted at an unnatural angle. Mani knew straight away. They weren't just lying there. They were dead.

Chapter 22

But something didn't add up. These bodies looked untouched—not the burned-out skeletons she had seen by the beach and in the boat. As Mani looked closer, she could see a brown-red trail of blood leading from the house to where the bodies lay. A smear—like a giant snail trail.

"Mani! Quick!" Leo called from downstairs again. Mani started. He must have seen them too. It was time to go again. There was clearly danger here. Mani hurried back down the stairs. As she passed through the living room, she saw hanging on the wall something she hadn't noticed before: a row of guns.

Leo was in the kitchen. He was excited. He had opened all the cupboards and a large walk-in larder and was loading tins and packets into an old suitcase on the table. Beside the suitcase was an open tin of beans in tomato sauce and every so often he crammed a sticky handful into his mouth.

"Help yourself!" he spluttered through a stuffed mouth, pointing at the tin with a tomato-saucy hand. "Then load up what you can. I've even found a can opener. But we need to be quick! I don't know how much time we've got... It feels like someone might still be living here."

"But—" Mani pointed out into the garden where the bodies lay. Her words stuck in her throat because now she noticed something else. The body nearest to the house—a man with his head turned away—had a dark-red bloody wound to the back of his head. Mani quickly pieced it all together. They hadn't died of the sickness. Someone had shot them.

"Come on, Mani!" Leo said again. "No time to waste! This is our chance to replace our rations!" He stopped to look at Mani. "What is it now?"

Before Mani could say anything else, a door slammed and the whole house shook. Then there was the sound of heavy booted feet in the living room and male voices that were deep and fierce.

Mani thought of the guns she'd seen in the living room, and the bodies outside. "Quick—hide," she whispered, quickly slamming the suitcase shut and dragging it and Leo into the larder, pushing them as far back as she could and pulling the door to behind them just in time.

The door was slatted, and through it they could see two heavy-set figures enter the kitchen. Mani and Leo crouched together beneath the lowest shelf at the back wall. Leo's shaky breathing sounded loud; Mani looked at him and placed her finger over her mouth. *Shhhhh!* she mouthed silently. Leo held his breath.

"You've been helping yourself again," one of the voices grumbled. Mani could see a thick grubby hand pick up the open can of beans on the table and slam it down.

"Ach, quit your whinging," the other, higher voice replied. "Just get your ammo and we'll get back out there."

"I swear, if I could do this on me own, I would." the deeper voice continued. "I'd get rid of you right now, you dishonest son-of-a—"

Mani and Leo watched through the slats. One of the figures went to the back door and picked up a metal box. The figure then moved back to the middle of the kitchen and paced around restlessly.

"I swear I left these cupboards shut," he muttered, slamming them closed.

And then Mani saw it again. There in the kitchen— the animal shadow that she'd seen at the beach and again in the forest. It had stopped right outside the larder door and was looking through the slats at her. Its ice-blue eyes shone like torches. Mani didn't know what it was, or what it wanted, but she didn't feel afraid. She squinted to see better. There was a grey snout and scruffy whiskers. A wolf. She gasped and watched helplessly as its shadowy shape turned and disappeared.

She looked at Leo. Had he seen it? A small voice forced its way out from the back of her throat. "Did you…?"

Leo, still holding his breath, was red in the face. *Shhhh*, he mouthed, rolling his eyes.

There was a noise in the living room, and the sound of something falling or breaking. "What the hell was that?" the deep voice rasped.

"You left the bloody door open," said the higher voice. "We've got company again…wretched wolves, after our food…Quick, bring your gun!"

Chapter 23

The two voices carried on into the living room, muffled and indistinct. Leo breathed out noisily. Mani scowled at him and then peered through the slats into the empty kitchen. All she could see—as if in a small frame at the end of the tunnel—was the door into the back garden. The wolf had distracted the men. Did it mean to help them? She thought of the guns and the dead bodies. And she knew. They needed to get out now—or else they might never get out.

Mani's hands were cold and damp. She could hear her own heart beating. It was getting faster and faster, like a clockwork toy being wound up. Her chest hurt, as if it might explode.

There was the sound of shouting from the living room and furniture being upturned. A deep snarl, and claws scraping over wood. The house seemed to shake around them. "Where is it?" the deep voice boomed. "Check upstairs." Then came the thud of heavy footsteps up the wooden stairs.

There was no time to waste. Mani stood up, pushing on the larder door, ready to go. But Leo pulled at her T-shirt, shaking his head. Mani shook him off and pushed at the door. Once again, she felt Leo's hand on her arm. He was still shaking his head and mouthing, *No*.

But Leo hadn't seen what Mani had seen. And there was no time to explain—about the guns and the dead bodies, or about the danger they were in. Leo would just have to trust her. They weren't going to die here. Mani looked at the suitcase Leo had filled. Some tins and packets had spilled out, and she now placed them quietly back inside and clicked it shut at the clasp. Then she picked it up by the handle.

She looked at Leo one last time, then she pushed the larder door open and stepped out into the kitchen. She moved quietly but deliberately, her feet padding silently across the wooden floor to the back door. She turned the handle gently, allowing it to click quietly, and finally she pulled the door open.

Mani was out.

She looked behind her. Leo had followed her out of the larder, but seemed to have stumbled. She stopped. Then Leo appeared suddenly at the back door. "Run!" he shouted, tripping forward and into the garden. Behind him, in the kitchen, the two figures loomed and voices were shouting.

Mani ran. She ran as fast as she could, the suitcase banging into her legs as she went. She ran past the blood trail, past the three dead bodies, past the dying vegetables and plants, until she reached a low fence that separated the garden from the encroaching forest. She threw the case over the fence and then leaped over herself, stopping to see where Leo was. He was stumbling and tripping, not too far behind. As he reached the fence, Mani held out an arm to help him over.

There was a gunshot and the wood on the fence splintered.

"Come back, you thieving vermin!" the deep voice bellowed across the garden. There was a crashing sound as the two figures lumbered after them, then a second shot rang out.

Mani kept running. She tore through the forest, weaving between the trees, on and on. Leo was following her, but was quite far behind. Yet Mani wasn't alone. Something was running right beside her. At the edge of her vision, against the wall of blurred grey trees, there was a low, elongated shape. A streamlined tail and ears packed down to gain speed. The sound of four paws galloping through the undergrowth. The wolf was with her. Running beside her. And this made Mani run faster and longer, until she could run no more.

Finally, she stopped. Her legs collapsed beneath her, and inside her chest a million sharp pains slashed like hot needles being dragged through her lungs. She flopped to the floor and leaned against a tree trunk, looking around her for the wolf.

Moments later, Leo came crashing to a stop beside her and lay on his back.

As their noisy breathing subsided, the silence of the forest filled their ears. Mani peered through the skeletal branches of the dead trees. The wolf seemed to be following her. Looking out for her. But where was it now? And what did it want?

"I think a wolf is following me."

Ooshaka was sitting opposite Crow. Crow had drawn a grid in the snow with his beak and they were playing tic-tac-toe. Ooshaka had already pressed a giant paw print into the top corner square. It was Crow's turn. He drew an *X* with his beak in the side-edge square below. Ooshaka sat with her head hanging over the grid, staring at it intently.

"Did you hear me? I think a wolf is following me." Mani tugged on Ooshaka's fur, but the bear was lost in thought.

Crow cackled. "Ha! The kid thinks *a wolf* is following her."

Mani ignored Crow. She carried on: "It keeps showing up. And then disappearing. But it's helping me, I think." Mani stopped. She was talking to Ooshaka, but it was more like she was explaining things to herself. Saying it out loud helped make sense of it. "I think it's good. A good wolf. It wants to help me. Us," she added.

"You keeping talking, kiddo." Crow winked. "You're getting there. Sometimes things that don't make sense over there—they make sense here." Then he extended his huge black wings and everything went dark. He whispered in Mani's ear, "Does that old wolf remind you of anyone?"

Mani looked through the darkness and found Crow's shiny eye. *Yes*, she thought. But she wasn't sure why.

Crow shuffled his wings back and it was light again. "I heard a rumour," he cawed, "that a fella who ends up here with unfinished business, well, he'll keep a-visiting your world until it's sorted." Crow winked at Mani.

Mani's head was hurting. She reached for Ooshaka and buried her face in her soft white fur.

Ooshaka was engrossed in the tic-tac-toe grid. Her calm concentration made Mani feel calm too. For a moment she forgot what she'd come here to talk to Ooshaka about, and what Crow had just told her. She was good at this game. The best. She played with her friends, drawing lines in the mud or scratching chalk lines into rocks. And she always won. She had a way. It always worked. She whispered in Ooshaka's ear, "The other top corner, the other top corner. And you'll win." The bear readied herself to make her move and then pressed a large paw into the top corner square, crushing the lines either side, as Mani had said.

Crow screeched, "Craaa-www-k! Come on! Two against one! Not fair!" He swept his black shiny wing over the grid and cleaned the lines away. Then he started to draw a fresh grid with his beak.

Mani burst out laughing, rolling on her back, and looking up at the sky.

"Tell the kid to show some respect!" Crow complained.

Mani's sides ached, and she rolled over the grid Crow had drawn. The sky above was blue and bright and made her eyes ache. Pictures flew into her mind now—dead seals, mighty waves, a row of guns, a swamp—and she could see herself running, gasping for breath, trying to get somewhere else, but never getting there. She stared harder at the sky and eventually the bright clear blue won, painting away the frightening images with broad strokes. "I want to stay here," she blurted eventually. "It's more fun. I don't want to go back."

Mani rolled over onto her tummy and looked across the ground at the endless, simple, white snow. This was easier, this nothingness. She closed her eyes and drifted into sleep, half aware of Ooshaka's body beside her, and half aware of the mask slipping from her head.

Chapter 24

"This morning, we feast!" a voice boomed over Mani's head.

She sat up, blinking. The mask was still on her head, although it had slipped round to the side and was pressing into her cheek. It took a moment to remember where she was. But she was still in the forest, having slept on the ground, on an old oilcloth, which Leo had laid out beneath her.

Leo was standing in front of her, bowing dramatically before a low rock on which he had placed a selection of food, the lids of the tins cocked open as if they were raising their hats. Low beams of early sun reached in through the trees and the metal from the tins glinted and winked. Either side of the big rock were two large, half-dead leaves, which Leo had laid out to sit on.

"A table for two, madam!" he offered. "In an enviable location."

Mani didn't know what he was talking about, but her stomach lurched at the sight of the food. She crawled over to the rock. The opened tins didn't exactly look like something you could eat—grey flakes and slimy yellow crescents—but one contained tightly packed silvery fish which looked edible.

Leo continued, "Today, madam, we have the catch of the day—a selection of locally caught tins—tuna and sardines—followed by a delicious dessert of *pêches en boîte*—tinned peaches, to you. Please, madam, have a seat." He extended an arm out to Mani, before lowering himself onto one of the leaves and gesturing for Mani to take the seat opposite. He took another large leaf and tucked it dramatically into the neck of his shirt, like a napkin.

Mani stayed crouching by the rock and reached out to take a tin.

They gobbled down the tuna first, followed by the sardines, and finished with the peaches. They ate quickly and in silence. To start with, they dug their hands in hungrily, but, as their stomachs filled, they slowed and extracted the sloppy, slippery peach slices with their fingers. Mani tipped her head back and poured the last dregs of sweet peach juice into her mouth.

Leo patted his stomach and let out a satisfied sigh. He leaned against a tree trunk and spread his tattered map out on the ground before him.

Mani rolled over onto the oilcloth and lay on her back. She'd left the mask there and now she picked it up. She looked across at Leo, staring at his upside-down face. "Thanks," she said quietly, and he nodded back at her. Upside-down, Mani couldn't work out whether his face was happy or sad.

Leo watched her for a moment, and his voice became quiet and thoughtful as he said, "You know, you remind me of my daughter."

Mani didn't reply, but she rolled over onto her tummy to listen. Leo's face looked different. Behind his scruffy beard, his mouth seemed to sag, and his eyes were shinier than usual. He blinked and shook his head, as if trying to get rid of a fly that was buzzing round his face. But there were no flies.

"She was about your age when she—when I—" He stopped, as if not sure of what he was saying. He looked away from Mani now. "She died…in a fire…and it was my fault. I try not to think about it…I keep busy with my work, but you…you remind me…" Leo pulled his glasses off and pressed his fists into his eyes.

Mani sat up now. She looked at the mask in her hands and stroked the feathers. She held it up for Leo to see. Could he use it? Would it help?

Leo looked at the mask. "How does it…?" he started to ask.

But something changed. It was like a door that had opened slightly inside Leo was closing; he squeezed his eyes closed and pressed his fingers into them as if pushing it shut. He stood up suddenly, tucked the map into his pocket, and paced around the oilcloth to the suitcase, which he snapped shut. He waved a dismissive hand in Mani's direction. "You know, when you put it on, you go into some sort of trance. You can't hear anything. That sort of stuff…it's not for me."

Mani looked round for her bag. She dragged it towards her by the strap and stowed the mask away as quickly as she could. She didn't want Leo to even look at it if he was going to be like that.

Leo carried on, "It's very odd." He cleared his throat and spoke loudly. "Nothing gets through to you when you wear it. You fell asleep with it on when we got here, and you slept all the way through to this morning."

But, before Mani could even decide whether to answer back, Leo had jumped to his feet and was looking over her head, his arms raised as if he might be about to fight something or someone.

"Don't move, Mani," he ordered. "Do—not— move," he repeated slowly, his eyes fixed on something behind her. "I've got this."

Chapter 25

"Stay where you are, Mani. Don't move. I said, DO NOT MOVE!"

Mani stayed sitting where she was, but slowly turned her head round to see what Leo was looking at. Shining out of the early morning light were two white-blue orbs. Those eyes.

"I've got this, Mani." Leo's voice was getting louder as he stepped past Mani towards whatever it was. "Stay back."

Mani watched Leo stumble sideways and reach for a branch that was lying on the ground.

"Go on! Shoo!" shouted Leo, stamping on the ground. He waved the branch over his head, but instead of shooing, the creature moved forward, out from the dark undergrowth.

The wolf.

"It must have smelled the food," said Leo. He stamped the ground again and shouted, "Go on, get out! *Shoo*, you beast!"

But the wolf carried on edging forwards. Its lips were curled back, and it was snarling. It wasn't going anywhere.

"Get behind the rock, Mani." Leo bellowed. "Quick! Don't just sit there. Hide!" He pointed at the large rock with the empty tins, but he lost his balance and fell backwards, waving the branch in front of him.

The wolf didn't wait. It moved further towards Leo, growling and drawing back on its hind legs, ready to attack.

Mani hadn't moved. The wolf seemed to be ignoring her and was only interested in Leo. But Mani wasn't afraid. Instead of retreating behind the rock, as Leo had commanded, she dropped onto all fours and started to move forward, towards the wolf. She didn't know why—it just felt right.

The wolf stopped and turned to look at her. Mani could see right into its eyes now. They were like two silver moons. Cracked and craggy, but illuminated by some kind of inner blue-white light. Mani almost felt like she was spinning around them.

And then Mani threw back her head and howled.

Everything stopped. The sound rose from deep within her being and seemed to dissolve high in the air and then fall all around them. It was like her voice was reaching out to touch something.

She could feel it in her whole body.

Within seconds, the wolf answered. It too threw its head back and howled. Its cry joined Mani's in the highest reaches of the forest above them, knitting together in one long siren call.

When the echoes finally faded, Mani and the wolf opened their eyes and looked at each other. There was something about the wolf, something in its intense, watchful air of authority, that Mani knew. And for a moment, as Mani stared into the wolf's eyes, she saw them change from white-blue to craggy grey, and there was a line of amber weeping across the grey iris to the white.

"Tatka?" she breathed. "Father? It can't be." And, in her head, she heard Crow: *Does that old wolf remind you of anyone?* But what did any of this mean? And, as she looked, she saw the wolf's eyes change back to blue-white.

Mani reached out and placed a hand on the wolf's back. Its fur felt strong and wiry. Then she let her arms wrap around Wolf's neck and sank her face into the softer white hair below his ears.

She turned to Leo and spoke quietly: "Don't be scared of him, Leo. I think he wants to help us."

Chapter 26

They walked in single file through the forest. Wolf was at the front, moving low and purposefully through the trees, his shadow weaving silently against the dense grey trunks. Mani followed, her eyes all the time on Wolf's sinuous back and tail. Leo tripped and stumbled along behind them, dragging the suitcase and grumbling as he went.

"This is nonsense. I'm not following a wild animal," he muttered, pushing his glasses up on his nose. "*I've* got the map." But he did follow, albeit tutting and spluttering into his beard as he went, trying to keep up with Mani.

Mani was happy to follow Wolf and, after a while, the tightly packed trees that had held them in a lifeless prison for so long started to thin out. All around them it was getting lighter, and the air was getting cooler. Jigsaw sections of clear blue sky started to become visible above them.

"He's leading us out!" Mani called back to Leo. "Look! Wolf has shown us the way out of the forest!"

They stopped and Mani looked ahead at the emerging view.

Leo pulled the map out of his shirt pocket. "Well, I'll be…But this can't be right," he said, unfolding the map and holding it up to the light. "How on earth did we get…?"

They both gazed out towards the horizon, past the last few dead trees. What had initially looked like a dull, grey, featureless landscape was in fact a huge wall of mountains culminating in three giant black peaks in the distance.

"But that's them," Leo carried on. "That's the Three Sisters." He put the map back in his pocket. His mouth hung open. "Well, I never…I'm not sure how, but we're back on the right track!"

Mani and Leo both turned to look at Wolf. He was sitting at Mani's side, surveying the new terrain through narrow blinking eyes. A light breeze rippled the fur around his ears, and his whiskers and nose twitched as he read the scents on the wind.

"Come on, then!" said Leo, placing an arm over Mani's shoulders. "Onwards!"

They walked together now across the open plain, Wolf all the time by Mani's side, in the direction of the mountains. It felt good to leave the forest behind.

Before long, an old road came into view. They headed towards it. It seemed to start far away in the distance, but came to a crumbly stop in the middle of the desert plain in front of them. It was totally broken—cracked and collapsed over the uneven landscape, like a ripped ribbon that had been laid over the unstable earth.

"Look at that," Leo breathed. "Even the land itself is broken." He held his hand over his brow and looked into the distance. "The ice melted, and everything solid went with it. All the structure...Do you see?" He stamped his foot on the crumbling tarmac. "A solidly engineered road, reduced to this."

But the broken road seemed as good a place as any to walk now, and they picked their way along its cracks and crumbles. Mani kept glancing at Wolf, who stuck to her side.

"Hey, Wolf," she said softly. "Who are you? Do you know me? Do you mean to help us?"

Leo turned sharply to look at Mani. "Oh, none of that...Nothing emotional about a wild animal. No talking to it...It'll tear your heart out in the blink of an eye if you get too close. It's all about survival."

Mani felt irritated again. Why couldn't Leo see anything? Why was he so against everything? She spoke now to the back of Leo's head: "We've come quite far, haven't we? Do you think my father's nearby? Do you think we'll find him soon?"

Wolf kept a steady pace beside her. The idea that he was somehow connected to her father felt right—but it

137

just didn't make sense, especially when she was talking to Leo. But the scientist didn't have any answers either.

Leo glanced back at Mani and stopped for a moment, pointing ahead. "See those three peaks. They call them the Three Sisters. And up there, between them—that's where the Ark is. That's where we're heading. We can't see it at the moment, but perhaps tonight, when it gets dark, we'll see the glass reflecting the moon and stars."

"Will he be there? My father? Do you think that's where he went, instead of coming back to me?" Mani probed, staring down at Wolf's powerful back and shoulders, and tough wiry fur.

Again, Leo paused. He spoke carefully now. "I believe there's every chance he's there, yes," he replied. He breathed in, as if he wanted to say more, but then shook his head and quickened his pace instead.

Mani felt Wolf press closer into her legs as she walked.

"So, best foot forward," Leo announced. "Another day of this and we'll be at the foothills—we've had three days on the road and we're already into the home stretch!"

They kept on along the road. The tarmac was riven and caving in, and in some places had split across the full width of the road, creating yawning fractures which they had to jump over. They came to an abandoned truck with one of its front wheels missing, making it tilt slightly to one side. It had been stripped, in the same way that

138

vultures strip a cadaver. Its rubber tyres, glass windows, and mirrors were all gone. Only the dusty blue-painted metal shell, which was being eaten by orange rust, and the interior seats and steering wheel betrayed its former life.

The sun was high in the sky now and bearing down on them. Mani stopped beside the truck. Her legs were aching, and her skin was hot. "Can we have a rest?"

Without waiting for an answer, she climbed into the truck and perched on the sloping driving seat. It felt soft beneath her, although the leather was hot and stuck to her legs. There was a dusty, fusty smell. She held the steering wheel and pretended to drive. Wolf circled outside, sniffing the ground around the truck.

Then she heard Leo cry out in a howl of pain. "What the—?" he exploded.

Mani looked out through the glassless windscreen and could see Leo was dancing about on the road, an arrow sticking through his forearm.

"Get out of my truck," a voice hissed at Mani. "Or you'll get one too."

In front of her on the road stood a girl. She had dark shoulder-length hair with a wonky fringe and was wearing army combat trousers and heavy black boots. Around her neck hung a pair of headphones, with a wire, cut and frayed, dangling against her chest. She was holding a bow and arrow. And she was aiming it at Mani.

Mani got out of the truck. She sidestepped towards Leo. "Are you OK?" she asked, glancing at his arm, but

139

trying not to take her eyes off the girl. An arrow was sticking all the way through Leo's arm, just below his elbow.

"Your truck? *Your truck?*" howled Leo as he hopped around, his eyes screwed shut. "What have you done to *my arm?*"

The girl shook her head impatiently. She strode towards him, snapped the back of the arrow off from one side of his arm, and then pulled the arrow-side out. He let out an agonized scream. Blood ran down his arm and dripped onto the hot dusty tarmac. She produced a dirty-looking rag. "Press this on," she ordered.

Leo pressed it on, wincing and swearing under his breath.

The girl fixed Mani with a hard stare. "You," she pointed at her with her bow, stepping away. "You need to get back to wherever you came from. You're sick. It's not safe. They'll kill you." She gestured with her bow back along the road, across the desert plain, back to the forest. "They're killing anyone who's got it. It's the only way." She pointed to her eyes. "Get away now, hide, and die in your own time. I won't say anything. But if you come any closer—" she drew back the string on her bow, ready to fire— "I'll kill you now."

Wolf was making tight circles around Mani's legs, and then moved forward, growling and baring his teeth at the girl. The girl stepped back, stumbling slightly, but then she steadied herself, lifted her bow, and pulled back an arrow. She pointed it down at Wolf, squinting over the length of it to aim.

But Leo stepped forward, in front of Wolf and Mani, still clasping his arm. "You'll have to take me first."

Mani watched as the girl lowered her bow slightly. She glowered back at the three of them. Then she blinked and, as she did so, Mani saw that her fearless stare wavered slightly, like a candle flame flickering in the wind.

Chapter 27

"What's that on your shirt?" The girl was looking at the Ark logo on Leo's pocket, still gripping her bow and arrow tightly and keeping it trained in their direction.

Wolf stood his ground, but didn't move further forward, crouching squarely in front of Mani, ready to pounce.

"Do you work for them up there?" She tilted her head in the direction of the mountains and the three peaks.

Leo nodded vigorously. "Yes, yes...and there's something you should know. We're on our way there because this girl, my friend here, is special. See? She's not sick. She's not dangerous. Yes, yes...she looks like she's got the disease, but she hasn't. Look—" Leo placed his good arm across Mani's shoulders and

142

grinned at the girl— "I can touch her. But I don't catch it."

Mani shrank beneath his arm. Then Leo stepped towards the girl, extending his hand. "Dr Leopold MacKintosh, research scientist for the Ark, at your service. We're on our way there—"

"To find my father," interrupted Mani, staring at Leo.

The girl glanced at her now, ignoring Leo's outstretched hand and still aiming the bow.

Mani felt Wolf at her side, his cool nose gently nudging her legs.

"Yes, yes…" nodded Leo. He waved his hand dismissively towards Mani, but he kept his eyes on the girl. "But, as well as that, we think the Ark will be interested in what our friend here has…what she might mean."

"Touch her again. Show me," she ordered.

Leo turned now to Mani. As he tried to lift his arms, the bloody rag fell to the ground. He embraced Mani in an awkward one-armed hug. His body felt bony beneath his thin shirt, and he smelled of dirt and dust and sweat and blood. With her head crushed to the side, Mani could see thick bubbles of clotting blood forming on his arm. They looked like they might burst at any moment. She remembered the small flecks of blood they'd inspected under the microscope back at the research station. It seemed a long time ago. She wished for the hug to be over.

"See? She's not sick." Leo's voice sounded muffled as he spoke above the top of Mani's head. "She's not like the others who have it. She's not dying."

The girl lowered her bow slightly and cocked her head to the side. "What's in the suitcase?" She pointed at the case, which was lying on the road in front of the truck.

"Oh, oh, that…," Leo said, releasing Mani now and wincing as he dabbed at the blood on his arm. "Well, we've got food…Enough to get us through our journey. Show her, Mani, don't hang around. Open the dratted thing."

Mani crouched down and clicked the clasp open. Inside the case were the rows of tins and the can opener, and a few bottles of water.

The girl stared at the contents for a moment. "And what's in the other bag?" She was looking at Mani's caribou-skin bag, which was slung across her body.

Mani's stomach flipped. Not the mask. She wouldn't give that away. Not to anyone. She opened the flap and held the bag open. "Just an old toy mask…and a broken torch," she murmured.

The girl peered in and nodded. "You sure she's safe?" she asked again, looking at Leo through narrowed eyes.

"Yes, yes. Come closer yourself, you'll see." He turned to Mani. "Mani, introduce yourself properly. Show some manners."

Leo was embarrassing, but Mani obliged; she held out her hand towards the girl, just as Leo had done. "I'm Mani," she mumbled.

The girl looked at her hand and then up at Mani. She had rich brown eyes, which hinted at a smile, but her

144

mouth remained pursed. She was a bit older and a bit taller than Mani. She didn't come forward.

Leo nodded encouragingly. "It's totally fine!" he urged. "Like I said, completely safe." He put his arm around Mani's shoulders again. Mani had an urge to wriggle free, but she stood still, her arm still extended.

The girl continued to look at Mani, and for a moment their eyes locked, and Mani had a feeling that the girl was seeing her for the first time. Not her electric eyes and all that they suggested, but really her. Eventually, the girl stepped forward slowly and held out her hand. She pressed it into Mani's. It felt cold and dusty, and her fingers were thin and light. But she didn't say *her* name. And Mani found herself thinking, *I've told you my name. Now, who are you?*

The girl dropped Mani's hand and turned to Leo. "Well, we *might* be able to help each other," she said. She slung the bow over her shoulder. "It's where we're heading too—the Ark. My stepfather is leading a group there—he has some stuff to trade." She pointed off the road and out over the desert plain. "We're camping nearby."

"Have you been here long?" asked Leo. "Has something held you up?" He grimaced as he pressed the bloody rag back on his arm.

The girl shrugged. "We can't get through the mountains. There's a pass, but he can't find it. Perhaps you can help?" She nodded at the logo on Leo's shirt again. "You being an insider?"

Leo nodded and patted his pocket, which contained his map. He looked out towards the three peaks.

The girl carried on: "And we can help you…sort that out?" She pointed at Leo's arm. Then she shrugged. "Or whatever. Follow me." She started to walk up the road.

Leo turned to Mani, but Mani was already following her.

"Come on, Wolf," she whispered. "Let's talk to her." But when she looked round, her heart sank. Wolf had disappeared. The girl was striding away quickly now— there was no time to search for him. Mani had to run to keep up. She wanted to talk to her. She wanted to call after her, *Wait! Slow down!* She wanted to ask her, *What's your name? Who are you?*

A short way up the road, the girl veered off the broken tarmac, out into the empty desert plain, towards some large rocks. They walked between the rocks for a while, which seemed to get bigger the further they went, casting heavy shadows across the dusty ground in the afternoon sun. Some were sunk into the ground where the earth had caved in, and some were cracked open like giant eggs. Finally, they came to a shallow valley along which a sea of coloured canvas stretched chaotically as far as Mani could see.

"This is us," the girl called back to them as they approached the edge of what looked like a small town. Row upon row of tents, of all different colours and sizes, sprawled in front of them. And between the tents all sorts of rubbish was amassed: old bikes, tyres, chairs,

146

doorframes—everything just dumped. There was a dreadful smell of rot and dirt and people and death.

Beside some of the tents were cages and trailers on wheels. Some were empty, and their open doors clanked in the light breeze. Others were locked shut. Mani bent and peered into one. Dogs of all shapes and sizes stared out at her, moon-eyed and submissive. One brown-black mutt with matted fur and milky eyes let out a whimper, and a ripple of barking and howling passed through the cages.

Beside the cages, children were playing in the dirt. They were dressed in torn clothes and were barefoot. They stared as Mani and Leo passed. A small boy with tufty brown hair and a dirty blanket which trailed on the ground behind him pointed at Mani's eyes and started to cry. A woman came out from a nearby tent and scooped him up; on seeing Mani's eyes, she gasped and ushered all the children inside. Mani could hear shouting from inside the tent, and before long another woman rushed out, and then another, followed by a gang of older children. And they were all pointing and shouting at Mani: "Get out! You're sick! Get out! You'll kill us all!"

The girl carried on walking through the city of tents, and a small crowd formed behind them, following them, shouting and screaming at them: "She's sick! Stay indoors! Get out, you vermin! Leave us alone!" But the girl carried on, until someone threw a stone.

Mani saw the stone skim the girl's elbow. And she saw her stop and turn slowly. They seemed to know her and quietened as she addressed them.

147

"Listen. She's safe. She's not sick. Not in that way. She—" she pointed now at Mani and Leo— "they . . . are here to help us." And she picked up Mani's hand from her side and lifted it in the air for all to see. "See? You can't catch it. She's different. I'm bringing her to my father. I'm bringing them to see Sköll. They are from the Ark."

At the mention of her father and the Ark, the crowd fell silent.

"I hope you know what you're doing, Tilde," someone muttered.

The girl kept Mani's hand in hers and held it high in the air, and finally the crowd started to disperse, muttering and mumbling, and people retreated into different tents.

Tilde is her name, thought Mani, as she allowed the girl to hold her hand again. It felt strong. And, for the first time since all this had started, since her world had fallen apart, standing with Tilde, Mani felt strong too. This girl was fighting her corner with her. And, for someone who only a few weeks ago had thought she was all alone, that felt good.

Chapter 28

"What do you mean, she's *safe*?" Sköll's voice was so quiet, it was almost a whisper. He was standing right in front of Mani, and his words slithered snake-like into her ears.

Tilde had brought them inside a large, circular, dark-green tent, and they were standing in a line in front of a table and an empty chair. Mani could just see through the layers of gloom to the back of the tent, where shadowy figures shifted and shuffled.

Sköll paced up and down the line. He stopped again in front of Mani. "She looks just like the rest of them," he sneered, bending and peering into Mani's eyes. In the metal buckle of Sköll's gun sling, Mani could see the lightning-crackle electricity of her eyes reflected.

Tilde looked down. She fiddled with the hem of her T-shirt. Mani was surprised at the change in her—

from the tough girl shooting arrows at them on the road, to this.

Sköll turned to her. "What do you mean, girl? Speak up! You said she's safe? Different? How?"

Tilde glanced sideways. "She's...like I said." She bent forward to look up the line and glare at Leo, who was fixing the rag more firmly around his bloody arm. "Help me," she rasped. "Tell him. Explain."

Sköll moved up the line to Leo, who looked thin and pale in front of this big, swarthy man dressed in army combat trousers, a heavy jacket with multiple pockets, and big black boots. He had long straggly hair that hung in clumps under a green peaked cap, and a patchy brown beard. Over his shoulder, he carried a gun. "You heard the girl," he said, frowning through the darkness. "Tell me."

Leo reached his good arm out to Sköll. "Dr Leopold MacKintosh. Research scientist at the Ark." His voice shook.

Sköll looked at his hand and laughed. But then he took it, like a lion picking up a dead rabbit to toy with. "Delighted to meet you, Mr Research Scientist," he said in a mocking drawl. Then his voice dropped again. "Now, tell me, quickly, why this girl is safe, and why I shouldn't just get rid of her on the spot, like we get rid of anyone with it. We're not in the business of dying from the sickness here."

Leo swallowed. "Well," he cleared his throat. "You have obviously noted that the girl displays a particular symptom of the disease that is currently endemic in our

150

land." He pointed to Mani's eyes. Mani glared back at him. Why was he talking like this? Using these long words?

Sköll paced in front of Mani, his hand fidgeting over the barrel of his gun. "Quickly, I said."

"But," Leo continued hastily, "importantly, she hasn't developed the sickness. She's safe around electricity and is non-contagious. See?" He touched Mani now, and she could feel his arm shaking. He went on, "It's my belief that such an important deviation in the progression of the disease should be brought to the attention of the senior scientists at the Ark, who are the only people who can develop a medicine to combat it."

Sköll listened. Mani shifted on her feet next to Leo. She didn't understand all these words Leo was using, but she knew he hadn't mentioned her father yet, which was really why they were here.

"So, you think the Ark can use her?" Sköll growled.

Mani spoke. "We're actually looking for my fath—"

"Yes, yes, we're on our way there," Leo continued, turning to her, shaking his head and pursing his lips together, signalling for her to shut up. "We've just had…well…a few setbacks. Let's say, it hasn't been a straightforward journey." He laughed nervously.

Sköll walked away from them. He rubbed his beard and then leaned on the table.

Mani turned to Leo now. "We don't need to stay here. We need to get on."

Sköll looked up. His head twitched and he lifted the gun from his shoulder holster.

"Shh," hissed Tilde. "You'll only make it worse. Honestly, you don't know what he's like." Then she spoke out loud: "Father. They have food also."

A smile formed on Sköll's lips, revealing black and yellow teeth, and Mani felt anger begin to grow inside her, like a germ multiplying and infecting her whole being. She fixed Sköll with her electric stare. One thing she knew for sure: they weren't going to stay here. She was going to find her father.

"Look. Here, Father." Tilde crouched down and opened the suitcase.

Sköll looked inside and scanned its contents. "Take it away," he ordered, and another figure slunk forward from the dark edges of the tent and dragged the case away. Mani slowly slid her own bag that she carried across her chest round to her back.

Sköll was now beside Tilde, speaking softly in her ear. "You did good, girl." He took her chin in his hand and stroked her cheek with his thumb. Mani saw her flinch, and noticed she kept her gaze down at the floor the whole time.

There was noise outside. Dogs—lots of them—were barking and whimpering and howling, and there was the sound of men shouting and a gun was fired.

A man rushed into the tent. "Sköll, sir. They need you. They've found something."

Sköll looked at the tent door and adjusted the gun on his shoulder. "You…," he jabbed a finger into Leo's chest, making him stumble backwards slightly and cough. "You come with me." Then he turned to Tilde. "And you, stay here with her. Don't let her go anywhere. I'll send for you when we're ready. We're not done here."

Sköll strode out and, with one last glance at Mani, Leo scuttled after him.

Mani and Tilde were left alone in the tent. And Mani was waiting. Again.

Chapter 29

Tilde sat cross-legged on the floor at the front of the tent. Her eyes were shut. Mani sat down opposite her and focused on looking anywhere but at Tilde. Everyone else had left, as far as she could see. After what seemed a long time, she sneaked a look at her. Tilde's closed eyelids were delicate and veined, like moth wings. Long dark lashes rested against her cheeks. She had pulled the headphones which she wore around her neck over her ears, and was nodding her head, as if listening to music, marking out imaginary beats with soft pulses of her neck. Mani could see the headphones weren't attached to anything—a torn wire hung down her front. She couldn't be listening to anything.

Mani kept looking, stealing new details about Tilde that she hadn't noticed before. Her long fingers were holding the frayed cord of her broken headphones and gently running along the green, red, and blue torn wires. She sat with her back straight and her shoulders square. She seemed strong. But Mani had seen that she was afraid of her father.

Tilde's eyes flicked open. "What are you staring at?" she snapped.

Mani jumped. She shuffled back on the floor, away from Tilde's fierce glare. She searched for something to say. "W-what are you listening to?" she stuttered, pointing at her headphones. Stupid question. She kicked herself, as her eyes moved down to the frayed wires still in Tilde's hand.

Tilde didn't answer. She just glared at Mani.

"Are you in the army?" Mani tried again, looking down at Tilde's camouflage T-shirt and combat trousers.

Again, Tilde didn't answer. She was staring into Mani's eyes.

Mani blinked slowly, uncomfortably. She knew what Tilde was staring at.

Eventually, Tilde shook her head and body, as if she was waking up, and pulled the headphones down from her ears. She glanced around the tent and straightened her legs in front of her. She looked at the door. Mani could see she didn't want to be here. She was like her—she wanted to be somewhere else. And, like Mani, she didn't know how to get there.

155

"No, we're not in the army," Tilde said eventually, looking back at Mani. "Whatever *he* wants you to think." Then she reached behind her and pulled a single arrow out of her quiver bag. She took a small penknife out of her pocket, unfolded it, and started to work the blade on the end of the wood, sharpening its point. "And he won't let me have a gun," she said, her eyes fixed on the point she was making. "So, I made this." She picked up her bow and laid it on the ground between them.

Mani was impressed. The bow was made from the branch of a tree. Knots and bark were still visible, but it had been expertly carved and polished and bent into an arc. She felt under her T-shirt and took her whalebone-handled knife from the leather holster.

"Can I help?" she asked.

Tilde looked at Mani's knife. She thought for a moment, and then took another unfinished arrow out of her long quiver bag. She shoved it across the floor to her. Mani picked it up. She watched how Tilde ran the flattened blade over the end of the arrow and nicked thin shavings from it to sharpen it. She started to do the same. They sat for a while in silence, carving the tips of the arrows.

Eventually, Mani spoke: "So, you're going to the Ark, like us?"

Tilde glanced up at her. "Too many questions," she said, but then immediately seemed to change her mind, and nodded. She looked at Mani. "What will *you* do? When you get there?" she asked.

"My father's there. We're going to find him," Mani poured out. But a shadow momentarily darkened her vision. "My mother's dead," she said, not knowing where it came from, or why she had chosen to tell Tilde.

Tilde carried on whittling away at the arrowhead. Her expression of deep concentration didn't waver.

Mani changed the subject. "Leo—the science-man—thinks his Ark science-people will be interested in me because of this—" she pointed at her eyes— "because I'm not dead; it didn't kill me, like the others." She shrugged. "And because…" She remembered what had happened. Leo had said she'd cured him, that she'd pulled the sickness out of him, that she was special. But she didn't say any of that, because, when she thought about it, it all sounded ridiculous.

"Congratulations!" Tilde laughed. "On not being dead!"

Mani laughed too, and they continued to work the wooden arrows in silence.

"My mother's dead too," Tilde said quietly, after a while.

Mani looked up at her, and for a moment she found her eyes. The whites were shining—tiny defiant specs of light in the gloomy interior of the tent.

"It's OK, I never knew her," she added quickly. She set down her arrow on her lap for a moment. "He's not my real father, he's my *step*father—and he's not in the army. None of us are. He just acts like he is. Says it's all about survival. Dog eat dog. Man beat man. He stole all the uniforms—and makes us wear them. Thinks it makes us a stronger unit. He stole the guns too, and he traps any dogs or wolves he can get his hands on. That's his plan—to trade them at the Ark. And I just have to go along with it."

She picked up the arrow again and dragged the blade of her knife over the tip.

"His plans never work." She dug the blade harder into the wood. "Nothing ever does. He'll be on to the next thing. And we'll be moving on again. And I just want…I just want…" Her knife slipped on the wood slightly and the arrow broke in two. The sharpened end fell to the ground. "Damn!" she muttered under her breath. And then she looked up at Mani. "I guess the difference between you and me is you want to find your father. I want to run away from mine."

Mani was holding two clumps of soft white hair in her hands for balance. She could feel Ooshaka's shoulder blades rolling rhythmically beneath her. The polar bear was walking slowly through the frozen land. She placed each huge paw down gently on the snow, as if the ground beneath her might break. The sound was of a damp scuff, like a soft brush hitting a hard surface. A *pfffft*, a *chssssd*. A soft cymbal sound played in a slow, rolling rhythm, driven by the bear's powerful body, with such a gentle but sure force that it felt like it might never stop.

Mani breathed slowly, in time with Ooshaka. She could feel Ooshaka's heartbeat in time with her own.

She looked down at the polar bear's body and stared deep into her dense white fur. Except it wasn't white really. Now she looked closely, she could see it was all the colours in between white: cream, grey, brown, green. A muted rainbow of off-white set against the pureness of the brilliant white snow.

Crow was sitting on Ooshaka's head. He was looking forward, quiet for once. His sleek black body rose and fell with each step Ooshaka took. He twisted his head and held a single oily eye on Mani for a moment. Then he winked and turned to look forward again.

Around them was cold, empty, endless white. And above them was crisp, endless blue. All Mani knew at that moment was the movement of Ooshaka's body, the up and down of Crow. And she liked it.

But Mani became aware of something pulling at her arm. Something telling her to lift the mask, to leave Ooshaka and Crow and the clean ice

159

world. Something was drawing her back, like there was something important she had to do but she'd forgotten what. But she'd only just got here. And things were confusing back there. She didn't want to go back so soon.

"I have to go," she said into the nothingness.

Ooshaka stopped.

Crow swivelled his head round and stared. "That's good, kiddo. You have to go, you go. *No problemo*."

Mani ignored him. Ooshaka lowered her body gently into a sitting position, and Mani slid down her back and landed with a puff of powder in the snow. Then there was a flapping of feathers and bones, a rustling and bustling of wind, and the Crow leaped—one-two-three—across the ground and flew away with a *Crawwk!*

It was quiet again. Mani could still feel a pulling or tugging on her arm. She didn't want to go. Here, it was peaceful. Free of worry. Free of the need to decide and do things. Free of the need to think about anything.

"I'll come back." She looked up at the bear.

Ooshaka blinked slowly. "You might," she said quietly.

"I will—I promise," Mani fired indignantly. How could Ooshaka doubt her?

160

The polar bear turned to walk away. And, for a moment, Mani forgot why she'd come here at all. And she just felt a tugging sadness inside.

Ooshaka was going. Why was Ooshaka leaving her?

Chapter 30

When Mani pulled the mask off, she found it was Tilde who was tugging at her arm.

"What are you doing?" Tilde whispered.

Mani blinked. She brought her focus back into the dark tent and saw Tilde's face looming above her.

She dragged the mask off her head and put it back in her bag. She was glad that Tilde didn't ask any more questions. She'd already told her it was only a toy—and she would keep it that way. What if Tilde said it was ridiculous, like Leo had done? She couldn't bear that.

"Come with me!" Tilde said. She was standing at the edge of the tent now, by an opening which she was pushing apart with one hand. A triangle of twilight sky sliced through the canvas and bathed her face in a pink glow. She looked strong again. "It's nearly dark. I'm bored. Let's go and do something!" She poked her head out of the tent, looking left and right. "There's something I can show you."

Mani stayed sitting, and now Tilde ran back to her and pulled her up by the arm. "Come on!"

As soon as they were outside, Tilde broke into a run, still holding Mani's hand.

There was no one else around. They ran past rows and rows of tents. Some had washing hung chaotically down the guy ropes, and there was a heavy smell of fire and cooking. They ran past dozens of rusty cages, all on wheels and all padlocked. Some contained what looked like boxes. Others had guns stacked upright like sticks. And some were packed full of dogs. As they passed, the sound of barking and whimpering and howling and scrabbling claws filled the air, betraying their whereabouts. And, in the midst of the mass of noise, Mani thought she could make out a single higher-pitched call: a wolf's howl. Her Wolf? She wanted to stop and look for him. Was he still around here? Where? But Tilde pulled her on.

She led her out of the tent city, past a field full of skinny horses tethered to poles in the ground. There were large rocks strewn all about, and they weaved through them until Tilde stopped in front of a particularly large and jagged one, with a sloped surface. She put one foot on its lower edge and looked at Mani, catching her breath.

"This. I want to show you this."

They clambered on all fours up the steep gradient of rock. At the top, Tilde stopped, and Mani joined her at the edge, looking at the sheer drop. They sat down and allowed their legs to dangle over the side.

Tilde was leaning back and gazing up and out into the distance. "Look," she said finally.

Mani looked at where Tilde was pointing. Stars were just beginning to poke through the darkening sky, like tiny torch beams through a dark-blue canvas. But in the middle was a cluster of glittering lights, brighter than anything else in the sky. Mani could see the faint silhouettes of the three peaks Leo had shown her earlier. And all the bright lights were coming from a plateau between the peaks. "The Three Sisters?" she asked.

Tilde kept her gaze fixed on the distance and nodded. "That's where we're going," she said solemnly. "The lights you can see? They're not lights. That's the Ark. It's made of glass. It's reflecting the stars." Her voice seemed to come from a different place now, as if she was dreaming. "When we get there, I'm running away. I hate him—my stepfather. I hate what he's doing. And I hate it here." She paused and drew a deep breath. "They say there is still a school running at the Ark. They say they want young people—that we're the future, that they're going to teach us. And I want to learn. I want to belong somewhere. I don't want to stay here with the guns and stolen stuff and caged dogs. Those dogs should be free." She looked at Mani now. "Like you. Like me."

Sitting next to her, Mani could feel her determination like an energy pulsing from her body. She thought about all that had happened to her over the last year. And in front of her was the Ark—glittering like a jewel in the darkening sky. A place of wealth, of learning, of hope, of science. Surely this was where her father was? It made complete sense. Leo was right. This was the place she needed to be. And Tilde was going there too.

A sound of jangling keys from below broke the silence. "Tilde?" a man's voice called sharply from the darkness. "Your father wants you in the mess tent. Now."

Tilde sighed. "We'd better go." She swivelled on her bottom and turned to Mani. "Don't tell anyone," she whispered, "about what I said." And she half crawled, half slid back down the rock to the bottom.

"I won't," called Mani after her, but Tilde didn't reply.

It was nearly completely dark now, and they ran to keep up with the heavy black boots thudding on the ground and the jangling of the keys. They followed the man back through the rocks and past the field of horses. As they reached the cages, the dogs began to bark and howl again. Mani stopped. She looked in at the ragged bodies and fur and gnashing teeth of the poor frightened animals. Some were wounded and had bloody gashes on their sides. Tilde stopped too and stood by her side. Anger rushed through Mani's arms and legs, hot and fast, and her heart was beating loud, like a war drum. How could they treat these animals like this? She wanted to unlock all the cages and set the dogs free.

"Tilde!" The man's voice came again. It was more insistent. "Sköll's asking for you. He wants you to bring

166

the girl. You don't want to make him cross. Get yourself to the mess tent now. He's waiting."

Tilde nodded. "We need to go," she said quietly. "We can't make him angry, or he'll put me in a cage with the dogs again. But we'll come back. These dogs need to be free—like us. This is just the beginning. I promise."

Chapter 31

The mess tent turned out to be more of a shelter than a tent. It was made of a large piece of sandy-brown canvas which had been stretched, but was now sagging, over four tall poles. A pot bubbled and spat over a fire, making the flames hiss. People were arriving to eat. They sat on stones, or on logs that had been dragged near the fire, bending over small tin dishes and shovelling the thin, grey-looking liquid into their mouths. It was properly dark now, but the orange light from the fire lit their thin faces and showed expressions of deep concentration as they scraped every last drop from the tins. Some looked up as Mani and Tilde arrived, and a nervous murmur rippled through the gathering.

Tilde held Mani's hand in hers. "She's fine, I told you," she said defiantly to whoever was listening. "Sköll knows all about it." She squeezed Mani's hand.

Sköll was at the back of the mess tent. It was dimly lit by a single, dripping candle. He was sitting on a long bench at the only table, leaning forward heavily on one elbow and swigging vigorously from a brown beer bottle. Beside him was Leo, clasping a bottle so hard his knuckles were white. Around his arm a fresh bandage had been tied, and blood from the arrow wound was just visible as a pale-red bloom through the white dressing. Mani noticed a pink rash was creeping up Leo's neck from below his dirty white shirt. He was sweating and his eyes flicked around as Mani approached, as if he was trying to avoid looking at her.

Sköll thumped his bottle down onto the table. "Ah— here you are!" He pointed to the bench opposite. "Sit!" Then, under his breath, he growled to Tilde, "I thought I told you to stay put, girl." He leaned back on his chair and surveyed Mani slowly. "So," he drawled, "I've been hearing all about this *very special* kid—" he drew out the words *very special* and laughed, then put his arm heavily across Leo's shoulders— "from this *top Ark scientist*."

Leo sank under the weight of Sköll's arm. He glanced at Mani. She could see he was trying to smile, but his lips were just pulled back and he was baring his teeth, like a snarl.

Tilde sat down silently at the table.

Mani stayed standing, staring at Leo. What was he doing?

"Food for our guests, Anders!" bellowed Sköll.

Mani heard the now-familiar sound of jangling keys, as the figure that had brought them here disappeared to fetch them food.

"Sit down!" Sköll commanded again.

Tilde looked at Mani and nodded her head very slightly. Mani sat down on the bench beside her.

Anders returned with three tin dishes. He placed one each in front of Mani and Tilde, and sat down beside Leo with the third. Mani peered into her tin; the spoon was resting on top of what looked like grey clots of matter floating in a thin, dirty liquid.

Sköll took another slug from his bottle and then raised it to Leo. "To friends in high places!" he toasted. "And to the Ark!" he added, winking at Leo and tapping the side of his nose.

Leo raised his bottle to Sköll's and clinked it. "The... the Ark, indeed," he stuttered.

Sköll put his arm around him again and leaned in to point at the logo on his shirt. Then he whispered to Tilde, dramatically, so everyone could hear, "Never forget...it's not what you know, my girl, it's who you know, and this guy, he's going to get us there...to the top!"

They all stared, now, at the fading Ark logo on Leo's shirt.

Then Sköll broke the silence. "Eat!"

Mani was hungry. The grey slop tasted of nothing and smelled only of the fire on which it had been cooked, but the warmth was welcome. And the feeling of it hitting her stomach was familiar. As she ate, something bloomed inside her. A full belly used to mean laughter. Closeness. A hand on her head, stroking her hair. A squashed kiss on her cheek.

170

Sköll's voice intruded. Mani opened her eyes and saw he was talking to Leo. Grey liquid was running out between the gaps in his teeth and down his scrappy beard. He wiped his mouth on his sleeve.

"We've all got something they want, eh? Guns and dogs—everyone needs guns and dogs, these days—for protection and for work, now electricity is screwed, and we've got loads of 'em. And they'll pay…Oh, they'll pay…" He pointed at Mani. "And you've got…," Sköll leaned forward to stare into Mani's eyes again. He reached out to her face and tilted her chin towards him.

Mani could smell his sour breath and see individual flecks of dust and dirt clinging to each clump of his long greasy hair and beard.

"You've got…a kid who don't get sick!" He dropped his hand from her face and roared with laughter.

Mani flushed uncomfortably.

Leo was bristling as he carefully set his bottle on the table, speaking softly through Sköll's mocking laughter. "Oh, no." He was shaking his head. "Oh, no, no." He fixed Sköll with a stern stare, raising his hand and wagging his finger, as he had done so many times to Mani. "You see," he began, "she's much more than that. So much more. Much more than all your dogs and all your guns. She is…," Leo picked up the bottle and drank slowly from it.

Sköll leaned back and listened. He had stopped laughing.

"She is…power," Leo concluded.

There was a pause, and Sköll bellowed with laughter again, thumping the table with each snort.

Leo frowned. He stood up, as if he were a teacher facing a class of rowdy pupils. He carried on speaking louder over Sköll's interruptions. "You see, yes, yes, she's not sick. And that's remarkable. But, there's something else." He turned to look at Mani and rested his hand on her shoulder. "One touch—and it happened." He spoke slowly. "I was sick. I touched her. She touched me. And she cured me." He sat down again now. "So, you see, it's not just that she doesn't get sick. She can heal too. She has power. The power to heal. Tell me, which of your guns or dogs can do that? And what will the Ark want more?" He folded his arms across his chest in answer to his question.

His words had painted themselves across the mess tent like banners and hung there for Sköll to take in. *Power. The power to heal.* Sköll's arm had frozen, the bottle midway to his mouth. He placed it back down on the table.

"What do you mean?" His voice had changed. It was low and controlled and laced with threat. Gone was the slurring and the laughter. "Come on, speak up, explain yourself."

Mani looked down. What was Leo doing?

Leo's voice quivered. The bottle fell over on the table in front of him and the dregs of a fizzing brown liquid spilled out. "I-I mean what I say…It happened. I had the sickness. I was dying. Only days left to live. All my colleagues—dead. And she, the only one in her village to survive, the last child—she cured me. I can't explain it. It was like she pulled the sickness out of me, somehow. The electricity is different for her—it's like the disease can't live on in her; she somehow contains it, or earths it, returns it to the ground where it came from." He closed his eyes. "My mission—our mission—to the Ark is to share this. It's an important discovery. Possibly the most important in the history of man, if we are to survive this. She has a special power to heal. The world is dying. The Ark will be able to use this. They have the science—the knowledge— to develop it, share it, stop the needless destruction. With the help of Mani, the Ark can save us all."

Once again, Mani felt her chin being lifted in Sköll's rough hands. She could see her eyes reflected in his wide black pupils, giving her away with the constantly crackling and firing lightning bolts. She wished they would stop. She didn't want to be special. She just wanted to find her father.

Leo stood up again and started to move away from the table. He stumbled slightly. "So, well, thanks for your hospitality." He motioned for Mani to stand up. "We'd better turn in. We'll make an early start in the morning." He turned to Tilde. "Perhaps you could show us to where we will sleep?"

Tilde flinched as Sköll now rose from the table too. He towered above Leo. "Oh, no. No," he growled. "You're not going anywhere." He leered at Mani. "Power? Power to heal? This kid's mine. To trade. With everything else."

And, without looking away from Mani, he clicked his fingers in the air. "Anders! Take them away—you know where."

173

Chapter 32

The cage was small. It rattled and clinked whenever Mani moved, so she tried to sit still. She needed to quell the sense of hopelessness that was seeping through her like black ink on paper. She was cross with Leo. She should never have trusted him. He was, after all, *cursed zientzia*, as her father would say. But what good did thinking like that do? It wouldn't get them out of here. She sat very still and thought. Because she knew that, if she allowed herself even a single movement, she might explode. She might grab the bars of the cage in which they'd been locked and shake and rock and wreck it and never stop.

The bars were thick and on all sides. A heavy chain had been wrapped multiple times through one side. A padlock hung from it. There was no way out. And Mani was alone. Again. Or she might as well be. Her father, her mother, Ooshaka, Wolf. Everyone had slipped away from her. If she was going to get any of them back, she had to be strong.

So now she sat motionless in the middle of the cage. She wrapped her arms around her knees and buried her head. And she tried to think of what could be done.

Leo was fiddling with the chain and lock, and feebly shaking the bars. Mani wished he would stop.

"It's no good. There's no way out," he was muttering under his breath. Then he turned and looked at her. "Oh, Mani, what have I done?"

Mani lifted her head.

Leo was kneeling at the side of the cage, the chain and padlock in his hand. "I've ruined everything. My big mouth. What was I thinking? There is no way out." He held up the padlock helplessly.

Mani looked at the chain that was wrapped around the bars, like a thick snake strangling its prey. What *had* Leo done? They were almost there. The Ark was in sight, away in the distance, the other side of these wretched bars, its bright starry reflections calling to her. So why were they now in here, locked away? Like dogs. To be traded. Mani looked at Leo's dirty white shirt, his ragged beard, and torn trousers. Who was this person? This science-man. Why had she agreed to this journey? Leo was right about one thing: he had talked too much—and this is where it had got them.

"I'm sorry, Mani. I'm so sorry," Leo said softly. "I don't know what came over me. I thought we were on the same side!" He yanked angrily at the chain again.

"But, even if we get to the Ark now, you won't be free. He wants money. He thinks they'll pay for you." He looked pale. "It's over, Mani. I have been so stupid. You're special. Why did I not think to keep that safe—a secret? Why did I not see that others would want you too?" He crawled across the mesh floor of the cage and sat in front of Mani. "But it's so wrong. This shouldn't be about money. It's about science. It's about saving the world. It was my one and last chance to get it right—and I've blown it."

Mani turned away from Leo to look out through the bars. It was always the same—science and saving the world. Never mind what's right in front of you. Had Leo ever really wanted to help her find her father? Had he every really thought about what she wanted?

In the next cage, Mani could see guns stacked upright in a row, like soldiers ready to march and kill. And, further away in the darkness, she could hear the scuffling of claws on metal in the cages where the dogs were imprisoned. They should be free, thought Mani. That's what Tilde had said. *Like you, like me.* But she was just like a caged dog now. Something to be sold and put to use. And somewhere out there was her father. She tried to focus and think logically. Her father would know what to do. Something heroic. Something wise and fearless. But what?

Leo shuffled to sit beside her. "I'm sorry. I really am so very sorry." He looked at Mani. "You're so brave, you know, and strong. You remind me so much of my

176

daughter. I should have looked after you, like I should have looked after her. How can I keep getting it so wrong?" He pressed his head into his hands. His voice was muffled as he said, "Perhaps it would have been better…if you'd never found me. I thought it was all over. I was dying. But you appeared that day at the research station, and everything changed. I stupidly thought you were mine—because I found you, and it was me who discovered your power."

Leo lifted his head now, his face drawn with anxiety. "And I lied. I promised to help you find your father, to get you to come with me, and I thought we might, but I could never promise that, because I don't know where he is. I don't know anything about him. I'm so sorry. I would do anything to help you now."

Mani stared at Leo. He'd *lied*? But did any of this matter? Whether Leo could help her or not, they were still locked in with no way out. And she had still lost everything. Almost.

Mani felt inside her bag. She still had the mask and the torch. And she still had her knife in its holster. She opened the bag and took the mask out, running her fingers gently over the feathers. Maybe Leo was right: it was stupid, the mask. What good had it done? Ooshaka hadn't given her any answers—not proper ones, at least—and Crow was just annoying. None of it helped. She looked at the mask, at its wooden, expressionless face and blank eyes. It gave nothing away, and right now this made Mani feel cross. She'd had enough of everything. There was no way out

177

of the cage. What good was this "other place" and the stupid mask? They couldn't help her now.

Mani decided she was done with Leo. But, more than that, she was done with the ice and talking polar bears and crows. From now on, she'd do all this alone. And she would go and tell Ooshaka right now that it was all over.

"Ooshaka! Ooshaka! Where are you?" Mani stamped her foot and puffs of white powdery snow clouded around her. She could feel the tiny ice particles melting inside her nose.

Almost immediately came a bluster of black wings and bones and feathers, and the sound of something landing and galloping a short way across the snow. It was Crow.

"Not you!" Mani yelled. "I don't want you. I want Ooshaka. Where is she? This is all too slow. I'm out of time. I've come to tell her."

Crow stopped in front of her. He shuffled his wings into his body and winked. "Gotcha, kiddo. Let's get this sorted. You've been kinda slow yourself. But you…you're young…But this is important! You've got a whole lot of destiny resting on those bear-cub shoulders. Crow's gonna help you. Come with me."

He galloped away from Mani across the snow, his wings spreading but never quite lifting him off the

178

ground. Mani followed. He stopped at a circle that had been cut into the ice—a portal into the deep sea below. The surface of the water was smooth like a mirror.

"Oh, she's down there, is she?" Mani demanded. She knew polar bears could swim. "Well, tell her to come up," she said. "Quick. I've got something to say that won't wait."

Crow looked serious for once. "Listen, kiddo, the bear—she's not gone anywhere. She's closer than you think. Just take a look." Crow bent his head over the water and looked down.

Mani copied, and, as her head peered over the edge of the ice, she saw a reflection of Ooshaka's face looking back at her. She couldn't help but feel glad at the sight of the bear. As she raised her hand to say hi, Ooshaka's reflection raised her big white paw at exactly the same time. Mani fell back into the snow. What did this mean? She scrambled up and bent slowly over the smooth surface of the pool again, and there was Ooshaka peering back at her again. Her mouth dropped open, and Ooshaka's did too.

"Are we all tooting from the same page at last?" Crow asked eventually. "You get it, now? The bear. She's been telling you. The answers are all in here." He bent forward and tapped Mani's chest gently with his beak. "Ooshaka—that dumb bear you love so much—is yours. Your spirit. Put it another way: Ooshaka—she's you."

Crow hopped around Mani and looked at her from the other side.

"That old mask—that helps you find it, your spirit. Your mother knew that. She told you the stories. You meet your spirit—your animal—whatever you need— but it all comes from you. Because it's all there inside you, kiddo. See? You have the answers. Your mother— she's gone—but she's there with you. And she's here in spirit. The eagle. You found her. You just had to look— into the world beyond."

Crow looked down into the water again.

"And you're lucky, kiddo. You got Ooshaka. That means you're special. The wisest and best of all the spirit animals—present company excepted, of course." He bowed now and shuffled on the ice. "You're young. Why should you know this yet? You came looking too soon. But I'm here to tell you now—spell it out—if that bear Ooshaka has all the answers, then so do you." Crow sidled up to Mani and whispered, "And, one day soon, I'll give you lesson two...You were born into this, kiddo, and the path you're gonna tread won't always be smoooooth! You're gonna need old Crow's help, now and then. You ain't seen the last of me!"

Mani looked again into the pool. She stood up, and saw the bear stand up on her hind legs. She smiled at Ooshaka, who she had loved since the moment she'd met her, and saw the same expression of shy courage and kindness reflected back at her. This was her? Had she known this all along? "But who are you, then?" she asked Crow.

Crow let out a throaty caw. He shook his body and extended his wings, two giant black curtains opening out onto the white stage. "Oh, *moi*? Old Crow?" He galloped one-two-three across the snow. "Oh, I just tell the stories, to help you guys make sense of it all," he called back as his wings lifted him up. "Stories. It's what you humans like. And, when everything's fallen apart, it helps you put it back together. And I'll be here to tell them—whenever you need me. Old Crow is hard to shake off."

And, as Crow rose into the sky, Mani felt a power coursing through her body. She stood and felt herself rise, as if on huge hind legs, and she found she was taller and felt stronger. An energy crackled through her limbs and she thought she might pop. Although she still didn't fully understand what all this meant, she knew one thing—she was ready.

Chapter 33

Mani looked at her hands. They were certainly her hands—small and brown and worn, with dirty fingernails—but something strange was happening. There was a growing energy inside her and it was pulsing through her limbs and into her fingers. It was as if, deep within her, a bow was being drawn back, ready to fire an arrow.

There was a noise behind her, an almost-familiar sound of jangling keys—the ones that had hung from Anders' belt and that she and Tilde had followed, only a few hours earlier, back to the camp. Was Anders coming back? If they acted together, could she and Leo overpower him? Was this a chance to escape? Mani looked at Leo now. His frail body was slumped forward, his head in his hands.

What would Father do? The old voice inside played again and again. *Tatka, what do I do?* One thing was for sure, he wouldn't look to this weak, defeated person sitting crumpled beside her for help. No. Her father would face the challenge head-on. And alone.

The sound of the clanking keys was getting closer and closer, and now Mani could hear soft footsteps. She stood upright, her head tilting slightly as it touched the top of the cage. She was ready. As soon as the key released the lock, she would move. And she'd be out. And she'd run, and finish the journey. She'd get to the Ark, and her father, with or without Leo.

But then came a voice, whispering from somewhere outside the cage. "Can I come with you?"

Leo raised his head. "Who is it?" he whispered back, shuffling to the edge of the cage and peering through the bars.

Mani could see a wonky fringe and a pair of headphones.

"It's me. Tilde," the voice answered shakily.

Leo, who appeared not to have noticed the bunch of keys she was holding in her outstretched hand, let out an incredulous splutter and looked at Mani, rolling his eyes. "It's just *her*!"

There was a pause. "I can get you out," Tilde said quietly. "But…"

"But what?" exploded Leo. "Haven't you and your father done enough already?"

Tilde stepped forward now, closer to the cage. She pressed her face against the bars and her eyes found Mani's. "But you have to promise that I can come with you."

183

Mani looked back into Tilde's shining eyes, and then down at the keys.

Leo continued his rant: "Where do you think we're going, then? It's you who got us into this mess to start with!" It wasn't helping.

"Not me," Tilde fired back, firm and insistent, her eyes flicking towards Leo. "That was Sköll—my stepfather. But *I* took the keys." She jangled them impatiently. "You can have them," she continued, pulling back from the cage. "But not until you promise me I can come with you."

Mani looked at her. She had come to free them. And Mani trusted her. Yes, she thought. You can come with us. You *must* come with us. She liked Tilde. And they had the same goal—they both had to get to the Ark.

But, before she could say anything, Leo was wagging his finger and snapping, "Pass those keys through, right now."

"Not till you promise," came back Tilde immediately, withdrawing her hand and the keys. "I'm not staying here. But it's not safe for me to travel out there by myself. We can all go together—look out for each other. I'm coming with you." She peered into the cage again and looked at Mani. "Tell the old man. Promise me now and I'll let you out."

Leo sighed impatiently, looking down at the bloody bandage around his arm, which had started to smell, but Mani held Tilde's gaze for a moment, and then answered slowly, "We promise."

Immediately, Tilde's hand reached through the bars. Mani took the keys. She quickly unlocked the padlock and unwound the thick chain until the cage door sprang open. The nearby cages were packed with sleeping dogs, and a ripple of uneasiness spread through them at the sound of the clanking lock and chain.

"We don't have much time," said Tilde, crouching at the open cage door. "The whole camp could wake at any moment, and as soon as Anders sees the keys are gone."

The nearby cages rattled and whimpering and yelping filled the air. Mani looked at Leo. He hadn't moved. He was still kneeling inside the cage, staring at the open door.

Tilde turned and disappeared into the darkness. "Quick," she called back. "Follow me."

Leo spoke quietly to Mani: "You go. I'm no good for you. I messed up. You're better off without me. Go with her. I'll stay here—I won't tell them anything."

Mani stopped and looked at him. She couldn't leave Leo here on his own. Not now. Not like this—a prisoner of these hustlers, with their guns and dogs. He wouldn't last a minute. And they had got this far together—they were nearly there. Besides, Leo was useful. He knew the Ark. He was part of it.

Not the zientzia, her father's voice sounded inside her. *Never trust the zientzia.* But Mani shook her head. "I need you to come," she said. And, in the reflection of Leo's broken glasses, she saw once again her own

185

eyes crackling and flashing electricity, a reminder of the sickness, and the world out there, and the danger they were all in.

Leo stared back at her. He looked small and pale and lost.

"Not because of this," Mani continued, pointing at her eyes. "Or whatever any of this means to you or anyone else. But to find my father."

Leo hung his head. "Of course, of course," he mumbled into his chest, as if correcting himself. He looked up at Mani and nodded. "I owe you that much. We will find him."

And, with Leo behind her, Mani stepped out of the cage. In the darkness ahead of her, she caught sight of a familiar, low, shadowy form sloping away. "Stay close, Wolf," she whispered. "I might need you."

Tilde was waiting for them at the edge of the camp; she was standing with two horses, holding each by the reins. The animals were thin—their ribs pushed at the taut skin on their distended bellies and their fur was crusty and matted. The dogs' whimpering was growing steadily into noisy barking.

"Hurry up," Tilde said, glancing back to the camp, which had started to glow with the fire of lit torches. She thrust one set of reins towards Mani and swung herself up onto the other horse.

"Here." Mani turned to Leo and helped him up. "Hold on here," she said, showing him the raised leather horn shape in the middle of the saddle. Mani hauled herself up to sit in front of Leo—the place her father would have sat when he first taught her to ride.

Tilde let out a high-pitched "Yip-yip!" and her horse skittered into movement.

Mani turned back to Leo. "Remember to hold on!" she said, before squeezing her heels into the horse's bony sides and echoing Tilde's "Yip-yip!"

Mani felt the horse start moving beneath her and it quickly settled into a rhythmic canter behind Tilde's. Her body began to move with the horse's as its hooves pounded the ground. *De-de-dum. De-de-dum. De-dum.* Leo held on behind. When she looked down, there was Wolf running along beside them.

The night air was smooth and warm on Mani's face and in her hair. The further they went away from the camp, the darker it got. The pounding hooves started to blur into a single thrum, the movement smoothed, and Mani felt as if perhaps they had left the ground and she might be flying. She shut her eyes. Was she back with Crow, flying through the night sky? From somewhere deep inside her, her voice broke free and she howled into the night, "*Ow ow owwwwwww!*"

And beside her Wolf answered, "*Ow ow owwwwwww!*"

Chapter 34

By sunrise, they had managed to leave the camp far behind them. The land had become craggier and the incline steeper. Finally, Tilde stopped. She let go of the reins and jumped lightly onto the ground. "Skit! Shoo! Away with you!" she shouted at the horse.

Mani looked around. Ahead loomed an infinite dark-grey wall of mountain, and somewhere behind that, no longer visible, were the Three Sisters and the Ark. In the sky, purple thunderclouds were rolling in and, even though it was early morning, the air was loaded with a muggy heat.

"This is as far as we can go with the horses," said Tilde, looking up at the mountainside. "I've never got any further than this. I think the track veers away in the wrong direction. If we're going to get there, it'll have to be on foot."

There was the distant sound of excited dogs yelping and yipping, and a whip cracking, as well as a deeper rumbling of wheels spinning across rough ground. Now and then, there was shouting—"Mush! Mush!"—and a fearsome roar—"Gaaaraaagwuhh!"

Tilde stopped and listened. Her eyes looked hollow. "It's my father," she whispered.

Mani strained to hear, but it was hard to pick out anything over the sound of her own heart beating furiously in her chest.

"They know we've gone." Tilde looked up at Mani and Leo. "They've followed us. The dogs must have our scent. We have to hide. If we're lucky, they'll try and catch the horses first."

Mani wiped the sweat from her forehead onto her arm. Where could they hide? She jumped to the ground and reached up to help Leo slide down the bony frame of the horse. She clapped and shouted as Tilde had done, "Skit! Shoo!" The horse whinnied and shied away. Mani looked up the mountainside. It became steep quite quickly but, about ten metres up, she could see a large shadow framed by spiky growth.

"Follow me," she commanded. She started to clamber upwards. The rocks were large and she had to stretch her legs to heave herself up. The heavy rainclouds rolled down the mountainside now and started to empty their load. Huge raindrops fell, hitting the rocks like a thousand hands slapping the hard surfaces, making them shiny and slippy. Mani ignored the grazes on her legs

189

and kept going upwards, determined to find somewhere for them to hide and shelter. They had got this far. They couldn't fail now.

Just as she had hoped, the shadow in the rock face turned out to be a small opening in the mountainside, which led into a cave. Tilde arrived just behind her. She was wet through, and her dark hair clung to her face in clumps, like seaweed on a rock.

"We can hide here," said Mani, peering out to see Leo, soaked through, slowly working his way up the rock. "The dogs won't be able to follow our scent now. The rain should have washed it away."

Tilde raised her hand high in the air with a nod and Mani clapped hers against it.

Entering the small, dry, dark space felt strange. It was only a short time ago that Mani had been waiting, alone and scared and hungry, in a dark cave just like this, with only one jar of pickled rat meat and a stub of candle left. The dark walls were illuminated suddenly by a flash of lightning, and then came a deep rumbling clap of thunder. The whole mountain shook. Leo arrived, soaking wet and heaving for breath. Another flash of lightning lit up his pale and frightened face.

Mani pulled him in further. They had to get well out of sight. "It's OK," she said. "You're safe now. We can hide here."

The cave was tiny, and they could only go a little way back before the ceiling got too low to even sit up straight. But the opening was shielded by a rocky outcrop and plant growth, and there was a small ledge from which Mani could look out without being seen. Leo lay at the back, his chest heaving with each wheezy breath.

The rain stopped as quickly as it had started and the thunderclouds cleared. There was a damp, earthy smell in the air, and Mani closed her eyes for a moment as the light breeze cooled her face. The dogs were close now. She opened her eyes. From the look-out, she could just make out that her horse had only gone a little way and was standing by the side of the track, almost where she had left it. It whinnied nervously as the pack of dogs skidded to a sudden stop; they were dragging what looked like an old snow sled that had been set on large cartwheels, and they sniffed excitedly, and yapped and nipped around the horse's legs. Mani craned her head around the rock to see better. Tilde came to sit beside her.

On board the sled were Anders and Sköll. Anders was seated, and Sköll was standing at the back, his raised right hand grasping the handle of a whip. Both had guns slung over their shoulders. They didn't speak, but Mani watched as Anders climbed off the sled and walked over to her horse and mounted it. The horse resisted, rising on its back legs and shaking its mane, but Anders yanked hard on the reins, pulling its head sharply to the side. Sköll looked around. His eyes tracked up the mountainside in the direction of the cave and scanned the rock face.

Mani held her breath. The dogs below jostled and whined feverishly, confused by the damp that was

191

evaporating from the ground beneath them, diffusing the different scents in all directions. Eventually, Sköll looked down. "Quiet!" he roared at the dogs. He strode around the sled and kicked the lead dog in the side. It fell to the ground whimpering, and the other dogs scurried around it, their ears flattened and tails tucked in.

Sköll and Anders exchanged words, but they were too far away for Mani to make out what they were saying. Then Sköll took his position at the back of the sled again. "Mush! Mush!" he cried. The dogs sprang into action and the whip snapped damply into the air. Anders kicked the horse, and it reared up on its back legs again with a whinny before skittering away. The sled started to move, disappearing along the track in a spray of stones and mud.

Mani breathed out slowly, then she and Tilde shuffled to the back of the cave to join Leo. It was dark there, and she pulled the torch from her bag, clicked it on and placed it on the ground. They sat down in a tight circle around the white light, as if gathered around a cold campfire.

Mani looked at the pale-lit faces of Leo and Tilde. "What next?" she asked, as much of herself as of her companions.

Leo blinked and straightened his shirt. "Good question. Well...," he glanced towards the entrance of the cave. "We should stay here and rest for a while. And then we should move on." He pointed at the torch. "This is very useful." He nodded at Mani. "And it's safe enough to use it here. I also still have something that might help us."

He took the map from his top pocket and unfolded it. The edges were now ragged, and as he opened it up the worn paper ripped in two. Leo muttered and laid it out carefully on the ground under the torchlight. Holding the pieces together with one hand, he ran a finger along the crumpled paper.

"We're somewhere around here, I believe." He looked up at Tilde. "Your father won't know this, but there's a series of tunnels that lead through the mountains to the Ark. They are old—and not so much used, these days. In any case, they have always been top secret. Security reasons." He tapped his nose. "At least that's one thing I managed not to blab. And, if I remember correctly...," he squinted and bent his head to scrutinize the torn centre of the map. "Yes, that symbol there—a bit like a shield— that should be an entry point into the system...We just need to locate it." Leo drew back from the map now and glanced from Tilde to Mani. "A half-day's walk should get us there, if we don't spend too long here."

The light from the torch stuttered now and yellowed slightly.

Leo folded the map. "Save the battery," he said to Mani. "We might need it again."

Mani switched the torch off. She lay down. The floor was cold and hard. In the dark, she could hear Tilde lie down opposite and, from his shallow wheeze, she could tell that Leo remained sitting. All were silent for a while.

"Must be time for breakfast soon?" came Tilde's voice eventually in the darkness. "What will you have?"

Ah, food … Mani thought, and her stomach curled restlessly inside her. Food. She took some time to consider, and finally decided.

"I'll have pancakes, with crowberry jam, and milk to drink," she said. Her stomach growled in agreement at the picture that came into her head of piles of steaming pancakes, dripping jam, and a glass of white, creamy milk.

Tilde laughed. "Mmmm, sounds good," she sighed. "But I think I'll stick with my usual—fresh bread with butter and jam, and hot chocolate to drink." She laughed. "Oh no! I'm dribbling!"

Mani laughed too. Suddenly, the floor didn't feel so hard.

"What about you, Leo?" Mani sensed Leo moving and lying down.

There was a pause. "Ach, well, you know," he muttered seriously, "it's a long time since I've actually chosen a breakfast…living on rations in the middle of nowhere…but…well…as you're offering, I'll have a full fry-up—eggs, bacon, sausage, fried bread, beans…and a nice cup of tea. Two sugars."

They stopped talking and allowed the thoughts of food and full stomachs to fill their heads.

In the darkness, Mani could sense Wolf had arrived before she saw him. She was getting used to him coming and going now—just a shadow, or the watchful white-blue orbs of his eyes, or the feel of his wiry fur beneath her hand. Sometimes, it seemed that only she saw him— or felt him—that he was here just for her. He settled down beside her and she ran her hand around his curled body, the strong pulse of his heartbeat joining her own. Wolf was looking out for her. And that felt good.

For a moment, she thought of the mask. It was at times like this that she would normally reach for it. When the emptiness came. When the hole left by her mother, and her missing father, was biggest, and when the danger of her falling down it seemed more likely.

But, today, Mani felt at ease. She had all she could hope for. And she left the mask in her bag.

Chapter 35

Had she not been running her hand along the dark-grey, shiny rock as she walked, Mani may not have noticed the entrance to the tunnel. She had been searching for what felt like ages. Wolf appeared now and then, his blue-white eyes glowing like lanterns in the dark shadows cast by the sheer mountain face, ever watchful. Leo and Tilde had gone on ahead. Leo's plan had been for them to work their way in sections along the base of the mountain, looking for the tunnel door he had shown them on the map. He thought it would be quicker if they split up to search separate sections. It seemed an almost impossible task, and Mani was so hot and thirsty and hungry, it was tempting to just sit in the shade of the sheer rock and give up.

Leo had described what the doorway *might* look like, but Mani hadn't expected it to be so hidden that it could be revealed by touch only. She had been walking slowly, half-heartedly dragging her hand along the rock face as she went, when she felt it. It was made of metal, but so similar in colour to the dark rock of the mountain, it was camouflaged. She felt the change though, as beneath her fingers it went from jagged rock to smooth metal. She stopped.

In the shadows, she could just make out a join in the rock face. Her eyes followed the line of a large circle shape, the same height as her, set flush in the rock. And, now as she looked more closely, she could see, stamped right in the centre, the familiar 'A' inside a squashed circle. The same symbol that was on Leo's shirt. The symbol for the Ark.

"This must be it, Wolf. This is it," she whispered. She traced her finger over the 'A' and mouthed the word *Ark*. They were nearly there.

"Leo! Tilde!" she shouted out. "I think I've found it!"

But, before she could shout out again, to hurry them back, a voice close to her said, "Stop." There was a crunching sound of footsteps and a figure stepped out of the shadows.

It wasn't Leo. And it wasn't Tilde. So, who was it?

The figure was dressed in a black jacket with a hood that was pulled right over their face. "Stop. It's not safe. Don't go there."

Wolf's body tensed and he lowered to the ground. Then came a crashing sound from in front, as Leo and

197

Tilde arrived back to see what Mani had found. Leo threw himself forward. "Yes!" He ran his hand over the metal door and then kissed the Ark symbol dramatically. "We're here! You've found it, my girl—well done!" He turned to Mani and beamed, but Mani was still looking at the dark hooded figure standing just a few metres away.

Leo turned to see. "Get away, you two. Stand back." Leo stumbled forward, extending his arms either side, as if to form a kind of barrier between the figure and Mani and Tilde. Wolf growled.

The figure sighed and pulled his hood back. Mani found herself staring into the eyes of a young man. But they weren't healthy eyes. Around the gaping pupils tiny lightning strikes of crackling electricity were firing. This man had eyes like hers. This man had the sickness. They stared at each other.

"Don't go there." The man edged round them to stand in front of the metal door, barring their way. "They're killing anyone with it. They'll kill you. I got out. It's not safe. Don't go there."

Leo moved to keep his position in front of Mani and Tilde. "We mean no harm to you," he said carefully. "Let us pass—and we'll be on our way. You can go your way and we'll go ours."

The young man paused for a moment, and then shoved his hands into his pockets. His eyes crackled white and red and purple. "Oh, you can pass," he said, without moving from his position in front of the doorway. "I'm just warning you—it's a bad place, they won't save you—"

"Nonsense," interrupted Leo. "I know that place. If anywhere is safe, it's the Ark."

The man turned his electric gaze on Leo. "You're wrong," he said flatly. "It's changed."

Leo shook his head impatiently. "Stand aside and let us pass." He pointed at his shirt, jabbing at the Ark logo. "I'm one of them. An Ark scientist." He wagged his finger now in the man's direction. "We work to save the world—we're the only hope. The Ark hasn't changed!" he snorted incredulously. "The world has."

The man moved towards Leo. He pulled his hands out of his pockets and pointed at his own jacket. It was also printed with the Ark logo. "I worked for them too. I was a lead scientist," he said quietly. "And I'm telling you—it's changed. They don't care. They're just interested in saving themselves. Power and money." He pointed at the doorway in disgust. "And they get rid of anyone who's in the way."

Leo looked at the man's jacket and then back at his eyes. "Look," he said eventually, "just move aside—you make your own decisions."

The man shrugged. He was younger than Leo and had short, dark hair. He turned to Mani, now. "I bet you think," he said softly, "that they've got a cure. That's why you're going there." He pointed at Mani's eyes and laughed. "Well, I can tell you, there are hundreds arriving every day. All like us." He pointed at his own eyes. "Everyone's saying, 'The Ark has a cure. They'll save us.' But it's all lies. It's a trick. There's no cure. I should know. I was part of it all."

As he continued talking, his words became slow and deliberate.

"Oh, yes, they'll take you to a clinic—and you'll believe them when they promise you it's to make you better, because they're the Ark and have the answers to everything—but you have to listen to me. If you go there, you won't get out alive. I'm one of the lucky ones. I saw it from the inside. And I got out." The man looked down.

"Are you alone?" Mani asked.

"I escaped with my family," he said, pointing at the doorway again. "We all got out." His voice became quieter and thinner—as if it might crack. "But I had to let them go on without me—they're clean and…" He wiped at his cheek angrily. "And I'm not safe. I'm dying. I can feel it. Burning from inside. I couldn't risk giving it to them. But at least it's on my terms, not the Ark's." He spat at the doorway.

Pulling his hood up over his head again and dragging it down over his face, he said, "I'm telling you, and I'll tell anyone who I meet. There's no cure there. Only death, for anyone with the sickness." Then he retreated into the shadows until all that was visible was a faint flashing of light, before he finally turned away.

Chapter 36

"Wait!" Mani called out suddenly, throwing her voice to the man, like a lasso into the dark. "I can help you."

Her heart was thumping and throbbing through her whole body; she could feel it in her throat and limbs and behind her eyes. Isn't this what Leo had been saying all along? That she had a special power? If it was true, then surely she must help this stranger who was sick, and who had lost everything?

Mani walked towards the man, reaching out through the dark mountain shadows to find his hand. She took it in hers. Then, there it was, the mighty sound—a cracking or clapping—and they were both thrown to the ground. She felt something coursing through her body and there was the powerful snapping sensation. She lay on her back and looked over at the man. He was sitting

201

up and blinking, but Mani could see straight away that his eyes had changed. They were a dark green. Clear of electricity. Mani had cured him.

Leo stood with his hands on his hips, his mouth hanging open, shaking his head. "Remarkable," he breathed.

Tilde was kneeling at Mani's side. She peered down at her. "Are you OK?"

The man felt his face and rubbed his eyes. He staggered over to the metal doorway. The surface was etched, but it gave a blurry reflection, enough for him to see his face. He turned to look at Mani, who was still slumped on the ground. "H-how…?" he stuttered, shaking his head and staring at her.

Mani felt weak through her whole body. It was as if someone had removed her entire skeleton and she was just made up of soft tissue and skin. Wolf lay next to her and gently nuzzled her fingers.

It was Leo who answered the man: "So you see, there *is* a cure. But the Ark doesn't know it yet. No one does. It's her—this child. She can heal."

"This is…," the man began, but he didn't finish. He stared at the ground and then looked up at Mani, his eyes brimming with emotion. When he spoke, his voice quivered. "I don't know what to say. Nothing would be enough." He crouched in front of her, taking her hands in his. "Thank you."

Then, suddenly, as if seized by an idea, he jumped to his feet.

"But it's obvious!" he said. "You must come with me! My family—they're following a trail. Others have gone before them—to a new settlement…a safe place…away from the Ark. They call it the Taiga." Then he crouched again in front of Mani and spoke softly. "The Ark is no place for you—especially you." He looked at her intently. "You must come with me. Now. You can make a new start—you all can." He turned and looked at Leo and Tilde.

Before Leo could answer, Mani pushed herself up with her elbows and shook her head. She looked at the doorway. They were nearly there, and she wasn't going to give up now. "We are going to the Ark," she said firmly. "My father is waiting there."

The man thought for a moment, and then he nodded slowly. "Well, then…at least take this." He felt in his pockets. "It's all I have. It's not much, just part of what I was working on, before I had to go…" And into Mani's hands he pressed a small box. "You can use it in the tunnel—but not before you're inside."

Mani took the box. It was made of rough wood, with a hinged lid and a small clasp. It felt light—it was so small, it didn't look like it could be holding anything of any real use, but she nodded and put it into her bag.

The man turned now to face the metal doorway and pressed his hand into the central section, forcing his whole fist into the imprint of the Ark symbol. There was a clanging sound and a small circular dial pushed forward. Using both hands, he wrenched the dial round. There was the mechanical sound of locks turning, and the whole door was released from the mountain. Crumbles of rock scattered on the ground as it clicked forward. The man heaved the door to the side, revealing the opening to a narrow circular tunnel cut roughly into the mountain. A draught of cool air seemed to breathe out from the dark earthy space.

Leo and Tilde moved either side of Mani, hooking their arms into hers as they pulled her to her feet. She stood up and a feeling of strength trickled back into her limbs. They shuffled together to the opening and looked inside. The walls were rough and crumbly, and water dripped from the roof. Wolf weaved between Mani's legs and took a position at the front.

"But, when you're finished there," the man said from behind them, "get out as fast as you can. Come and find me. My name is Teodor. When you leave the Ark, follow the river west, till you get to the Old Man of the Taiga. Just remember that—the Old Man. You'll find us in the forest there. Remember my name: Teodor. You will always be welcome wherever I am. I owe you my life." As he pushed the door closed behind them, he whispered, "Good luck."

And then there was total darkness. Mani blinked. It was so dark, she couldn't tell whether her eyes were open or shut. They stood together in silence.

Leo spoke first. "Well, it's certainly dark. Mani, that torch—do you still have it? Will it work?"

Mani felt inside her bag for the cylinder shape of the torch. She flicked the switch. Nothing.

"Never mind," muttered Leo. "We'll have to use our hands. We can feel our way along the wall…it's narrow enough…if we take it slowly."

Mani heard Leo step forward, but she wasn't so sure. Could she step out into this dark emptiness? Who knew what was out there? Was it a trap?

Tilde nudged her. "Come on, we can do this," she whispered. "We've got to."

Then Mani remembered the box Teodor had given her. He'd said to use it inside the tunnel. She took it from her bag and felt around for the clasp with her fingers, opening the lid.

Rising in the darkness out of the box came a small orange light. It fluttered up, and as it rose it seemed to grow, until it was the size of a large lantern suspended above their heads. Mani could see Leo and Tilde and Wolf again in the orange hue. They were all looking up, turning around and around as their eyes followed the light that now circled above their heads.

"A firefly!" breathed Leo. "He gave you a firefly. But it isn't a normal one." His mouth hung open. "It's shining brighter than I've ever seen a firefly shine before—he must have been working on it at the Ark before he left. It's really quite remarkable."

Mani stepped towards it, and as she did the firefly moved away along the tunnel. She followed it. Tilde was behind her, and then Leo. And, with each step they now took, the light stayed ahead of them. With Mani at the front, they moved in a line through the tunnel.

After a while, a pinprick of white light became visible in the distance. As they continued, the pinprick got bigger and bigger, until it was a full circle. Soon, in that circle, they could see blue sky and white clouds. The firefly's light faded, and it returned to sit on the box, which Mani still held in her hand. She opened it and the firefly dropped inside. "Thank you," she whispered, shutting the box and placing it back in her bag.

They stopped finally at the tunnel exit, standing together, side by side. In front of them, rising mightily into the sky and glinting blue glass and steel in the glare of the silver daylight, there it stood: the Ark.

Chapter 37

"Wow…it's beee-yooo-tiful!" Tilde's voice sounded heavy and dreamy.

"Well, yes," said Leo, his neck craning back and his eyes scanning the huge structure that dominated the sky ahead of them. "It's good to be back…I think."

Mani didn't say anything. She held her hand above her eyes to try to reduce the glare from the monstrous building that seemed to be hanging above them. So, this was the Ark. Somewhere inside this steel and glass monolith must be her father.

Mani's eyes scanned the structure for what might be a way in. It looked impossible. She could see, rising importantly from the plateau between the peaks of the Three Sisters, two massive gates. On top of the gates, two thick curved silver buttresses swept upwards, like muscular arms reaching to the heavens. Between them they held a large silver globe, as if ready to smash down onto anyone who dared approach. And on the silver globe was emblazoned the "A" inside the squashed circle: the Ark.

Despite their size and power, the gates were ornately decorated with curling and twisting silverwork that seemed to thread and wind infinitely upwards. The delicate design allowed, here and there, a glimpse of what lay behind. It was a neat, ordered landscape. In the centre were two rectangular, neatly edged lawns, which flanked a central walkway. This was lined with evenly spaced but heavily laden fruit trees. The walkway led to a bridge over a wide churning moat, and then up and up to another set of dark gates, which were crowned with long steel spikes. Either side of these gates were two thick, tall towers. And, behind them, yet another cascade of steps rose upwards to the Ark building itself.

Mani shivered. Protected within all those layers of spikes and moats and bridges and walls, the Ark thrust out from the mountains like a warship. It was made up of three enormous triangular sections that gave it the shape of a boat, or "ark". It was constructed largely from glass and metal, and the expansive panels reflected the metal-grey clouds so clearly, it made the building seem almost part of the sky. It was as if the whole structure was suspended above the earth, its mighty bulk powering high above the confusion and chaos below. It was as if the Ark had become part of heaven itself.

"Just beautiful," breathed Tilde again. "I can't believe I'm actually here."

Mani blinked. "So, how do we get in?" She looked at Tilde and then at Leo. Then she looked around her. *And where's Wolf?* she thought. A feeling of panic gripped her. He'd gone again. *Come back! I need you.* Just a swoosh of his tail or a distant howl would do. Just to know he was near. Where had he gone? Wolf belonged by her side.

As Mani scanned the surroundings, searching for him, she started to see the world they had arrived in properly. The whole place was buzzing with life. Right in front of them, people were rushing and bustling in all directions. It was some kind of market day. There were stalls and huts and tents and tables. Around the edge of the market, hewn into the rock face itself, were shadowy doorways, hung clumsily with canvas awnings held together by bones and ropes. Everything seemed broken and falling down. Tables were wonky and stalls were in fact little more than a few pieces of rough wood bound with rope. Stallholders advertised their wares by shouting in sing-song voices:

"Rats on sticks!"

"Fresh fish eyes!"

"Rabbit feet!"

"Last few!"

"Get them while you can!"

A fight started, with people shouting and screeching, and bodies writhing on the dusty floor, trying to punch and wrestle each other. A single gunshot rang out, the sound ricocheting between the mountain peaks like deathly church bells. And then there was silence. People stopped moving for a moment and turned to stare. But, slowly, the market activity started again, like a clockwork machine being wound up, and the rush and bustle carried on as if nothing had happened.

"We go straight to the gates," said Leo firmly, in answer to Mani's question. He looked up at the seemingly impenetrable gates. "And we tell them who we are and why we're here." He turned to Mani. "I'll do the talking. Tell me, what's your father's name? We can start the search straight away." He combed his hand across the thin wisps of hair on his head, and then touched the Ark symbol on his shirt.

Mani looked gratefully at Leo. "My father's name is Ervik," she said. It felt odd saying his name out loud, because she only ever called him Father, or Tatka. Calling him by his name made him seem further away. That was what *other* people called him—in hushed voices of respect, and sometimes fear. Ervik, the leader. Ervik, the elder. Ervik, the strong, wise one who everyone turned to for guidance. They didn't ask Ervik for friendship. Ervik kept himself at a distance, so he could take difficult decisions. Mani felt confused. Was she looking for her father, or Ervik?

"Ervik," Leo repeated. "Right. Let's go and find him."

Chapter 38

As they started to walk, an old man sidled up to them. He was wearing a long leather coat and a dirty cloth hat. He was filthy, and when he opened his mouth, his bearded grin was toothless.

"New arrivals?" He sniggered and swung open his coat. From an inside pocket, he pulled out what looked like a handful of tickets. "Free passes—into the Ark?" he whispered. "That's where yer headed, in't it?" He smirked. Then his clouded gaze rested on Mani, and his face screwed in horror as he saw her eyes crackling with electricity. The old man fell back, spluttering, "Get away! Yer not wanted here! They're trying to make this place safe. Get out, you filth!"

Leo stepped forward, pushing the man aside. "Don't be ridiculous!" he said, his gaze fixed on the Ark.

The old man stumbled away and was soon lost in the crowds.

"Follow me!" Leo ordered, and he ushered Mani and Tilde forward a few steps, before stopping. "But… oh dear…you'll need to cover your eyes. We can't risk anyone else seeing you and getting the wrong idea." He rubbed his chin.

"It's obvious, isn't it?" said Tilde, pointing at Mani's bag. "She can put on her mask. The eye holes are in the wrong place—too high up. You can never see her eyes when she wears it!"

"Yes, yes, of course!" beamed Leo. "Excellent. Put on the toy mask. I will guide you, if you can't see. At last, it will be of some use! If anyone asks, I'm your father— we're a family, just arrived. We've come a long way and we're looking for shelter. Tilde, you might as well put those on too." He pointed at the broken headphones that she always carried. "Yes…you're my children, right? Keep it up until we get inside, and then we can explain everything properly. But we don't tell anyone anything until we're right inside that Ark building. Let me do the talking. I'm not taking any chances, now."

Tilde put her headphones on and started tapping her foot in time to an imaginary beat, as Mani took the mask out of her bag. She looked at it for a moment— plain and wooden and white. There was no time to sit with it, or to summon the lights. She put it over her face. It felt hard and the eyes were indeed too high up to see through.

Leo hooked his arm through Mani's, gently pressing her forward. "Just stay with me," he muttered.

They started to forge a way through the jostling and bustling crowds, towards the silver gates of the Ark. Although Mani could hear her footsteps crunching across the mountain rubble, and the mask felt cold and hard against her face, she also had a sensation of being half pulled back into the now familiar world of white snow, blue sky, and yellow sun. It felt good. She wanted to be there. She was striding forward. Her legs felt powerful, and her breath steamed in front of her. Her feet were firm and sure, like big paws padding against the ground. And, when she shook her head, her whole body moved and a deep rumble came from her chest. She could no longer sense Leo or Tilde, but she wasn't walking alone. Above, she could see Eagle circling in the sky, and in front of her stalked Wolf. A rainbow arched through the sky and dissolved in the whiteness ahead, sending stripes of colour in all directions. Mani felt powerful and purposeful and brave. It was a feeling of coming home. And now she could do anything.

Then, suddenly and violently, the mask was ripped from her face.

Eagle and Wolf were gone, and she was back on the rubble in the darkening shadow of the Three Sisters and the looming bulk of the Ark, a thin and hungry girl in a tattered T-shirt and shorts. Around her, the crowds fell away, and she was surrounded by horrified faces and gaping mouths. In front were three imposing figures, dressed head-to-toe in black protective suits. They were wearing clear goggles, which revealed only their eyes behind the black hoods and breathing masks. Guns were slung over their shoulders. Mani's feeling of power and purpose was stamped out, like a candle flame being extinguished.

"Infected," came a stern voice. The hooded face loomed nearer, and Mani flinched as a pair of impassive goggled eyes stared into hers. Two of the black-clad figures moved to either side of her. Their suits were made of a rubbery material and squeaked as they moved. The voice from the man in front came again. It sounded strange and tinny through the breathing mask. "All new arrivals report to the registry office. Infection is fast-tracked straight to clinic."

Leo stepped in front of Mani, his hands motioning in the air for them to stop. "No, no—you've got it all wrong!" he exclaimed. "We're not new arrivals; I belong here." And he pointed to the logo on his shirt. "And she's not infected, she just looks as if she is. In fact, we're—"

The figure pushed him to one side easily and turned away. Mani realized now that Leo looked absurd. His clothes were dirty, his hair and beard long and tangled, and a long dark scab was slashed across his arm. His glasses were clouded, one lens cracked. And he was very, very thin. Mani felt pincers on each of her arms as she was half lifted, half pushed into motion.

"Hey!" Tilde shouted as the figures marched off, taking Mani with them. "Leave her alone!" She was running after them. "She's my…my…my sister! We're going to—" But they weren't listening.

Mani tried to look behind her, she tried to shout, but it was all happening too fast. There was nothing she could do. And the last thing she saw as she was dragged away was her mask lying on the dusty ground—battered, dirty, and indifferent.

Chapter 39

"Name or number?" It was a woman's voice. But what did she mean? People only ever had names, didn't they?

Mani had been marched into the heart of the Ark building, and she was now standing in a glass-walled room in front of a long metallic desk at which another faceless figure in full protective clothing was sitting. On the desk were two neatly stacked piles of books. Behind the desk were floor-to-ceiling shelves and another door. The two figures that had brought her here stood either side of her.

Where were Leo and Tilde? And why had Wolf deserted her again? Mani had been bundled and dragged here alone. Eventually, Leo and Tilde's cries had died away, and she had given up trying to say who they were and why they were all here together, because nobody was listening to her, and every time she spoke or resisted, they pushed and poked her harder.

"What do you mean?" she asked.

"Were you given a number when you registered?" the woman asked, breathing heavily through her mask. Mani could see beads of sweat dripping from her brow, but her eyes were expressionless.

She stared. "My name is Mani," she said coldly.

The woman sighed and lifted the top book from the left-hand pile, opening it. "Write your name in here." She swivelled the book round and pointed a gloved finger at the bottom of the page. It was headed *Clinic Register* and displayed a list of names, numbers, and dates, and some other writing that Mani couldn't decipher. "At the bottom," the woman rasped through the mask. "Just your name, then. I will add the other details." She handed Mani a pen.

Mani stared at the list of names in the thick book. Who were all these people? And what had happened to them? Her hand hovered with the pen over the bottom of list.

She paused.

The woman stood up from the table and turned away to get something from the shelves behind her. Mani set the pen down. What was this list? She started to flip back through the pages. Name after name after name. All these people had been here? Had they all been sick? Had the Ark cured them all?

Then, suddenly, she froze. Could it be? Was that—? She started to flip the pages back. Her hands were shaking. She scanned each page furiously to try to find it again. Had she imagined it? She needed to slow down. She couldn't see anything with her mind racing so feverishly. The woman was sorting something on the shelf behind her and her back was turned still. Mani carefully ran her finger down each page as she read the names—and, finally, there it was. She hadn't imagined it. In strong, blocky handwriting that she recognized immediately: *Ervik*.

Somewhere in the distance, she heard a wolf howl.

Mani felt like she had been punched in the stomach. "My father—he's here!" she burst out.

The woman swung round and looked at her. The rubber suit was too big and she moved clumsily.

"Th-this is h-his name," Mani stammered, pointing at the line in the book, hardly able to breathe. "See? Ervik? That's him. I know his handwriting. This is my father. Where is he? I must see him. Is he being treated for the sickness? Is he in this clinic?"

"There are lots of Erviks," sighed the woman. The plastic on her mask steamed up slightly and her eyes were looking down at the book.

"But, no!" Mani exploded. "This—" she pointed down at the book— "this is him. It's his writing—I know it. Where is he?"

The woman had turned her back on Mani again. She picked a bundle of clothes from the shelves. "You can ask when you go through," she said quietly. She handed Mani a set of pale-blue garments. "You'll need to put these on now, and leave your things here." She nodded at Mani's bag.

"But my father! I must see him! Which room is he in?" demanded Mani, looking at the door and then at the woman, whose eyes closed for a moment behind the goggles. "Where is he?" Mani demanded again. "I thought he was lost. I came here to find him. I have no one else. You have to help me! Take me to him!"

The woman's eyes softened slightly. "Please," she said quietly. "I'm not permitted to discuss anything with patients. Just ask when you get through. But get changed first."

Mani couldn't wait any longer. She quickly pulled off her T-shirt and shorts, which were little more than rags now, and left them in a pile with her bag. "Will I get this back?" she asked, setting the bag down as she pulled on the rough pale-blue pyjamas.

The woman didn't answer.

Mani paused for a moment, then quickly pulled the top down over the holster with her whalebone-handled knife. She would keep that on under the hospital clothes— she might need it. But she could leave the bag—what did it matter? The mask was lost and the torch was broken. And there was no time for questions or even to think. Getting through to her father now was more important than anything. She was so close. She couldn't wait to see him.

"You can go through now," said the woman. She stood up to open the door behind her, which led directly onto a long, descending spiral flight of stairs.

The air was cool and smelled damp as Mani descended, and it got darker and darker.

Another rubber-suited figure was waiting at the bottom; this one had something long strapped across his back: a gun. He nodded and opened another door.

Mani stepped into a windowless room. A single candle flickered on a ledge at the far end. Suddenly, a young man rushed at her, shouting, "Don't come in here! Get out while you can! This is a set-up—they're not curing us. We don't get out of here alive!"

"Silence!" ordered the guard behind Mani, cracking the end of his gun against the concrete floor, before retreating and closing the door behind him.

The young man quietened immediately and sat down. Someone else muttered, "Sit down and be quiet. You're only making things worse."

As Mani's eyes grew accustomed to the dim light, she could see a dozen or so people sitting on two benches facing each other. They were all wearing the same pale-blue pyjamas, and they were all sitting with their heads hung low, staring dolefully into space. But something was clear straight away: they all had one thing in common. The room was lit further by the crackling electric energy buzzing in the rows of eyes that turned to look at her.

Mani froze. Different thoughts were lining up in her head and connecting, as if along a wire. And now, illuminated, she saw the terrible truth.

She thought about what Teodor had said at the tunnel. He had warned them not to come here. He'd said the Ark had gone bad, that they took in the sick to "treat" them, and that no one got out alive.

And she thought about her father. He hadn't come back to her in the cave. He had disappeared. But Mani had seen his name on the list here—at the "clinic"—written in his own handwriting. All those months of waiting. And her father had never come back. Because he had been here.

She thought about what this young man was saying right now, in this sealed room at the Ark, where she and all the "sick" people had been brought. And, in one awful moment, everything made sense.

Mani's father wasn't just missing. He hadn't disappeared. He had been brought here because he was sick. And he hadn't got out. He was dead. They had killed him.

Chapter 40

Dead. My father is dead. The words drummed a solemn beat inside Mani.

He was dead. Not missing. And he had been killed. Not by the sickness, but by the Ark.

I could have saved him. If I'd got here sooner, I could have saved him.

This thought now turned over and over inside Mani's mind. The unfairness. Nausea washed through her. She'd had the power to save her father. But she'd got here too late. She had waited too long.

But she could still do something. She looked at the closed doors in the sealed room she was now locked in. These sick people were all awaiting the same fate, as her father had done. Had her father just sat here, or had he fought? Mani closed her eyes, unable to bear the thought.

I'm different. I have a special power. I can save them. But Mani knew she had to be quick. She looked along the two benches. These people had given up already. The only life in them was in their eyes, where electricity raged, killing them slowly, but the Ark wanted rid of them now. It wasn't trying to make them better.

But it wasn't too late.

"I have something to say," Mani started. "It sounds strange, but it's true. You probably think I'm sick. Like all of you. But I'm different."

"Oh, sit down," grumbled a woman. "Everyone thinks they're different. Everyone deserves 'special treatment'. Get over yourself. There's no hope for us. Just sit down and wait. Let us have our last moments in peace."

Another man turned and looked up at her, shaking his head, but Mani stepped forward. Nothing was going to stop her. Not now.

"I've travelled a long way, searching for my father." Her voice sounded clear and strong, and seemed to fly around the room, carried on the wings of a pride she hadn't realized she felt. Yes. She'd come a long way. And she had tried to find her father. *She had tried.* "And now I know he is dead. But I could have saved him."

"You heard," came another voice. "Nobody cares about your story. Go quietly, like the rest of us. It will hurt less."

There was the sound of muffled sobbing. Then, the door opened. Two faceless figures in rubber suits and masks, and carrying guns on their backs, came in.

"Next," a low voice commanded. They pulled the young man who had shouted at Mani earlier to his feet.

He resisted, dragging back with all his weight. "No! Spare me! I have a family. They don't know—"

"Wait!" Mani's voice came loud and clear from the end of the room.

Everyone turned to stare at her.

"Watch," she said calmly.

She stepped to the bench and knelt before the person closest to her. She looked up into the face of an old woman. Her skin was brown and heavily lined, and grey curls framed her face. She was staring at the floor, her eyes flashing and crackling red and white angry lines. Mani gently reached for one of the woman's hands, which she held folded in her lap, resting lightly against the pale-blue fabric. Her knuckles were knotted and her skin lined with raised veins, like the branches of an ancient tree.

And then came the mighty snap. Mani was thrown across the room to the ground. She could feel the cracking and moving of energy as the sickness somehow shifted from the old woman's body to hers.

Almost immediately, there was a commotion. Lying on the floor, waiting for recovery, Mani sensed movement all around her. There was the noise of doors opening and closing, and of rubber suits moving and squeaking. There was shouting.

"She's cured!" It was the young man's voice. "Look! Look at her eyes." Then his voice was closer, speaking

224

in Mani's ear, and he was kneeling next to her. "Will you…? Will you fix me too?"

Mani rolled her head to the side and nodded, raising her hands to meet the young man's. Again, there was the huge cracking of power shifting, or something moving. And more shouting. "I am…I'm fixed! I'm cured!"

Now, the whole room was filled with noise and shouting. Different hands were grasping Mani's, and her whole body contorted with snap after snap after snap, as each person came and touched her, her body pulling the sickness from them.

Both doors were fully open now, and there were people running out and up the stairs. Mani could hear the squeaking of rubber suits around her, and low talking amid the shrieks of joy.

And then Mani was being lifted and carried on her back, up some stairs, through long corridors with shiny ceilings. All the time, there was talking and fussing and excitement.

"Find Leo," murmured Mani. "And Tilde. Leo can make sense of it. Tilde can explain. They can help."

But, before she could say anything else, a black curtain descended over her eyes, and she passed out.

Chapter 41

When Mani came round, she was sitting in a large chair with a long back. Her legs didn't reach the floor, and her hands were bound to the arms with plastic cable ties.

She blinked. Everything looked fuzzy. She was in a huge hall. The ceiling was high and made from glass, and it seemed as if the grey clouds outside were hanging right inside the room. There was a spiral staircase on either side, leading up to a series of platforms and doors into other rooms.

The wall to her left was made entirely of giant glass tanks. They were all different sizes and filled with a clear blue liquid; suspended in this liquid were the perfectly preserved dead bodies of different animals. Animals from the past. Extinct animals. Mani could see an Arctic fox; it was caught in the liquid, as if it was running.

There was a snow hare on its hind legs, boxing at the glass, and a fat puffin, staring blankly out, its rainbow beak muted by the blue liquid in which it was trapped. In the centre, the largest tank housed a baby killer whale, its body curved as if changing direction in the ocean; it looked as if it might be about to burst out of the glass. Nearest to her, in the smallest tank, a white dove was spreading its wings, suspended in flight, its beak wide open. Mani could see that the animals were dead, but they looked trapped, as if they had been frozen the very moment they tried to escape.

On the wall to her right there were three doors, each with a sign above. Mani's eyes scanned the words. The first read *Frozen Zoo*, the second *Seed Bank*, and the third *Pollinators*.

In front of her was a long, wooden, polished conference table, and behind that was a large, wooden panel displaying a portrait of a woman dressed in white, with white hair and piercing blue eyes. In the centre of the long table was a series of objects: a human skull, a transparent box containing a giant purple butterfly pinned through its abdomen, and a basket piled high with the same red fruit that Mani had seen on the trees outside.

Right in front of Mani, on the floor, was a huge white fur rug made from the pelt of a polar bear. Its four legs were splayed either side, and its opened mouth displayed a row of broken teeth. Its eyes, though peeled open, were opaque and dead. Mani felt a roll of anger drum inside her again.

She realized she wasn't alone. A figure perched at the edge of the conference table. It was the same woman as in the portrait—and her blue eyes were fixed on Mani like lasers. She had short white-blond hair, and was wearing a neat white jacket with a large shiny brooch on the lapel—the distinctive symbol of the Ark. Beside her stood a man in white overalls. He wore thick glasses and held a clipboard, on which he wrote as she spoke.

"So, you're the child who can save lives, are you?" Her voice was soft, almost a whisper. She stood up and clicked across the shiny floor towards Mani, bending to peer into her face. She smelled clean and sharp, of citrus and soap. She stared into Mani's eyes. Then she stepped back, folding her arms. "Remarkable," she murmured, before turning and resuming her perch on the edge of the table. "Go on, then. Why don't you tell me all about it?"

Mani tried to pull on the plastic ties that held her to the chair. She didn't like this woman staring and she didn't want to answer any questions. "Where are my friends?" she asked, as she twisted and turned her wrists. "Where are Leo…and Tilde?"

The man bent to whisper something in the woman's ear. She nodded, without allowing her ice-blue gaze to leave Mani. Then he disappeared behind the wooden panel and Mani could hear a door clicking shut.

"Do you know where you are?" the woman asked, reaching over for the basket of fruit and popping a shiny berry in her mouth. "Perhaps, if I explain a little, you might be more inclined to talk…My name is Dr Eliza Graves."

Mani didn't say anything. Her body slumped into the chair.

"You're in a place of scientific excellence—one of the branches of the Ark. A privileged place. A seat of the highest learning." She clicked across the room now towards the dead animal tanks and looked up at them. "The world has changed," she continued, her back to Mani. "You know that. We are in trouble. Humanity is on the verge of extinction."

She turned and walked back to the table, picking up the human skull and cradling it in her hands. She held it up to Mani.

"Our New Mission here is to harness the power of science to save our species. To save the world. Like the Ark in the story, we are creating a safe place, for knowledge and discovery. We are building it on higher ground, locking our precious knowledge away from the death and destruction of our world, until such a time as it is safe—" she placed the skull down on the table and picked up the butterfly, showing it to Mani— "for our metamorphosis."

Mani looked at the butterfly, pinned inside its box, and imagined it beating its wings and flying away.

"We keep these dead animals preserved as a memory tool—so we know what they looked like, and how they moved." Eliza gestured to the other side of the room, to the three doors. "We have the knowledge—the instructions, if you like—to rebuild them. We have the building blocks of life. We have saved seeds and bees, and can revegetate the planet." She looked now at the butterfly as if admiring a family photo. "We can re-create life. Future generations will thank us for keeping them safe, for destroying the bad and protecting our precious knowledge."

Mani squirmed. "Is that why you are killing people?" she shot at her. "Is that why you killed my father? Was he 'bad'? I could have saved him. I could have saved others. They weren't 'bad'."

Eliza leaned with two hands across the table and fixed Mani with a steely glare. "So, it's true? You can save people? You can cure the sickness?" She leaned further forward. "Speak. Before it's too late. Do you know how lucky you are to be here? To have an audience with me? The sickness has killed many, many people, and continues to do so. If you have some power, or some knowledge, you owe it to the Ark, to your planet, to your fellow humans, to share it."

Mani said nothing. But, in the vacuum of the great hall, she heard the sound of a door opening and closing, and footsteps rushing in.

Chapter 42

eo and Tilde appeared from behind the wooden panel. The sight of Leo's thin, slight, shuffling frame, and Tilde's confident booted stride, was a relief. Mani let out a long breath. They were here. They looked dirty and scruffy against the shiny clean surfaces of the great hall, but they were here. Her friends.

Leo placed his hand on Mani's head and ruffled her hair. He bent to speak to her. "Are you OK?" he said gently.

Tilde stood beside her. She was craning her head back and looking all around. "Wow. So cool. Have you seen all this?" She pointed at the animals in tanks. "I've read about these—but I never thought I'd see them for real."

"I'm glad you appreciate them." Eliza's voice slinked across the empty space; it was smooth and caressing, but carried a hint of threat, like a cat's claws sheathed inside silky padded paws. She clicked towards them, her arms folded.

Tilde looked at Eliza and glanced up at the portrait behind her. Then she turned back to gaze at the animals. "I love it!" she breathed.

Eliza nodded approvingly.

Leo, who had been fussing over Mani, stood up straight now. "Dr Leopold MacKintosh," he announced, extending his hand towards her. "Ark scientist. You may be familiar with my work?"

Eliza looked Leo up and down, and then slowly turned and walked away. She moved around to the other side of the table and sat at the central chair. She placed her hand on the table and drummed her nails on the glass. When she spoke, her voice was strung with impatience.

"Dr Eliza Graves." She fixed Leo with her laser-blue eyes. "No, I'm not familiar with your work, Dr MacKintosh, but you have my attention. Please, I understand you are acquainted with the child...and you say you have been studying the Terra Electrica sickness? Tell me what you know. What data have you gathered? Histology? Pathology? I assume you've been keeping records?"

Mani felt Leo's hand on her shoulder. It was warm and steady. He ignored Eliza's questions. "Why have you tied her up like this?" he asked, pulling at the plastic around Mani's wrists.

232

Eliza's face flickered with irritation. Her voice became taut. She took a sharp breath in. "I'm sure you know, doctor, this is a potentially valuable asset. One with huge implications for the survival of our world. But she's also dangerous. Until we know what we're dealing with, we won't take any chances. Now, if you've got anything to tell me, I would advise you to do so right now. As an Ark scientist, I'm sure you don't need reminding of the New Mission and your duty. What do you know about the Terra Electrica? And how can this child help us?"

"Terra Electrica? Is that what they call it here?" Tilde blurted, looking at Mani and Leo and raising her eyebrows. "Terra Electrica sickness—?"

"Enough!" interrupted Eliza, but then she softened. She held up the basket of fruit and turned to Tilde. "Try the fruit," she soothed. "It was created by our scientists from the knowledge we have stored here—an experiment, with rather delicious results."

Tilde looked at the fruit. She walked around the table and Eliza pulled out the chair next to her. Tilde took a berry from the basket and ate it. She didn't sit down.

"This won't do at all…No…no…," Leo had raised his hand and was wagging his finger. "No…no…She's a child, not an 'asset', not a 'discovery'. Her name is Mani. And she's lost everything. She is unique and precious. You can't tie her up like a prisoner. Have you lost your mind?"

Eliza stood up now. Her blue eyes glinted and her jaw stiffened. "The Ark's New Mission, Dr MacKintosh,

233

remember…? Or have you been away too long? The preservation of knowledge. The pursuit of progress. If you believe in anything else, you're not fit to wear the Ark uniform." She pointed at Leo's filthy shirt and what remained visible of the embroidered 'A'. "I am the New Mission leader now, and I keep it tight. Nothing gets in the way of progress. If it does, I pluck it out and destroy it. One rotten apple can destroy the whole barrel." She picked a berry from the basket and rolled it between her thumb and forefinger, before crushing it, allowing the red juice to drip slowly onto the table.

Leo stepped towards her and spoke in a voice that Mani had never heard before. It was deeper and richer— as if it had been warmed by something. "I used to think like that—that the only thing that mattered was my work. It's why I brought Mani here. Why I—we—made this journey." He looked at Mani apologetically. "But I know now. And she taught me. Science and knowledge are the future—but they are nothing if we don't use them to look after each other. I've made a big mistake in my life. I lost my daughter. She died because I put my work above everything. It was my fault. And I'm not about to make the same mistake again. I'm not asking you; I'm telling you, politely, to untie my friend, and treat her properly, or you answer to me."

Eliza threw back her head and laughed. But the laughter dropped away as suddenly as it started, and a black look fell over her face like a heavy curtain dropping over a stage at the end of a play. "Call yourself a scientist?" she snarled. "You've lost your edge, doctor. And I don't have room for people like you in the Ark. Not anymore. We need black and white thinking. No emotion—no colour."

She clicked her fingers, and from behind the wooden panel two black-clad figures with guns and goggles appeared.

"Take him," she commanded. "You're of no use to me, doctor. In fact, you're getting in the way." She turned to look at Tilde, who was still standing beside her. "You can stay—we can use bright kids like you."

The guards took Leo by the arms.

"Stop!" shouted Mani. And, as that single word came out of her mouth, something very strange happened.

Chapter 43

"Stop!" Mani shouted again.

Something was happening inside her. It was as if all the anger she'd been feeling was transforming into a feeling of power. It was coursing through her limbs and into her hands, and there was just a single word repeating inside her head: *Ooshaka. Ooshaka. Ooshaka.* With an explosive thrust, Mani broke free from the handcuffs that held her to the chair and stood—free— in front of Eliza in the great hall. The guards were still dragging Leo away across the floor.

"Leave him alone!" she cried out.

At her fingertips lines of light and electricity had appeared, which seemed to gather and shoot from her hands. She threw her arms forward and in one single strike, a powerful bolt of lightning zagged out in front of the guards and, as she moved her hand, a dark smouldering line was drawn on the ground in front of them. Mani froze. What had just happened? She looked at her hands and then at the burn line on the ground.

The guards paused for a moment. They were looking at her hands too, but there was no visible weapon that she could be using. Grunting, they carried on dragging Leo away, but with more urgency now, trying to distance themselves from whatever it was Mani was firing at them.

"I said, *leave him alone*!" repeated Mani, her voice full and strong.

"*I* said, get him out of here!" roared Eliza, pointing at Leo and walking towards Mani. "I'll take care of the child."

This was too much. Mani was not having this. The power was rattling at her hands—she didn't know what or how, but it seemed to be driven by her fury, and she realized she could direct it. She pointed at the glass panes and fired another lightning bolt, and another and another, and then she dragged lines of electricity in a full circle around the whole room. The glass fractured into a million little crystals, before they cracked outwards and fell like snow to the ground. Cold air rushed through the now-empty steel frames into the great hall. Then cracks appeared in the tanks that housed the dead animals, and the blue liquid started to seep out. Mani watched as a small crack in the largest tank snaked across until the whole glass case broke and the blue liquid flooded onto the floor. The two guards holding Leo stumbled back, releasing him. The giant carcass of the baby killer whale came crashing out of the case and thumped to the floor, sliding towards them and knocking their legs from under them.

Mani turned to Eliza. "You people killed my father," she said quietly. "I will not let you do the same to my friends." Then she raised her hands to the portrait behind the table and dragged a long line of electricity across Eliza's outstaring face. The portrait started to burn.

Eliza carried on walking towards her. "You're wrong, child," she said, pulling what looked like a syringe from her pocket. "And *I* make the decisions around here. It's a mistake to mess with me."

Mani shook her head. She pointed now in front of Eliza and fired a bolt to the ground, dragging the electricity across the floor as she walked around her. A circle of flames imprisoning her, Eliza was trapped.

"Seize her!" Eliza screamed to the guards, who were cowering on the floor at the edge of the room.

"Run!" shouted Tilde.

Mani started to run. Leo stumbled behind her.

"Don't just sit there! Go after them!" Eliza screamed again and again to the dazed guards.

Mani, Tilde, and Leo were running now. And there was no stopping them.

Chapter 44

The only visible way out of the great hall was the two spiral staircases that wound, via a series of platforms, from the ground to the ceiling. And the only direction to go was up.

Mani led the way, clattering up the metal steps, leaping two and three at a time when she could. She waited at the first platform for Leo and Tilde to catch up.

Leo was struggling. His skin was a doughy white and covered in a shiny film of sweat. His filthy shirt clung to his thin frame and his breathing was shallow and wheezy. "I'm not sure I can go on…," he spluttered. "You go. I'll hold them off. I messed up, Mani. Let me do this for you, at least."

But Mani took his hand and pulled him on, and Tilde went behind, pushing him forward and catching him when it looked like he might fall back.

"Come on, old man," she cajoled. "We're not leaving without you."

The final staircase led to a small platform with a single door. They paused, squeezing together on the narrow landing to look back down. The great hall was in chaos. Fire was raging across the floor. The portrait of Eliza had burned out, leaving a gaping black hole where her face had been. The long table was roaring with flames, and the polar-bear rug had ignited and was spewing out a dense black smoke; only its head and gaping jaws remained. Blue liquid continued to jet and spray from the shattered glass tanks, where the animals now slumped, but nothing seemed to quell the fire.

More guards arrived, and Eliza, still held within the circle of flames Mani had created, screamed orders and pointed up to the ceiling platform where they stood. In the middle of everything, freed from its glass prison, sprawled the carcass of the baby killer whale, now trapped in this new fiery hell.

"That was so cool," Tilde said to Mani, lifting her hands and examining them closely. "How did you do it?"

Leo leaned against the railing and heaved for breath. He nodded, swallowing and coughing. "An interesting progression, you might say…"

Mani didn't know how she had done it. The power was inside her—but she had driven it. And it had come from her anger and the unfairness of all that she had seen. The Ark was killing people—and her father was

240

just one of its victims. These Ark scientists were ruthless. They weren't the heroes Leo had said they were. Would Eliza have had Leo killed too? Just because he was of no use to her? Mani refused to stick around to find out.

She pushed open the final door, behind which a narrow ladder led up to a small hatch door overhead. Mani climbed to the top of the ladder and twisted the lock open. She poked her head through the hatch and was immediately hit so hard by a thump of wind, it made her gasp. She hauled herself up, then helped the others through after her.

They had arrived at the very top of the Ark. As Mani looked around her, she could see the dark forms of the Three Sisters looming on all sides. Deep-grey storm clouds billowed impatiently around their peaks.

Mani walked to the nearest edge. She peered over and her eyes ran down the sheer glass side of the Ark and straight into the seething waters of the moat far below.

Tilde and Leo followed and stood either side of her. They all looked down together. They could see from here that the moat was in fact a river. The Ark had been built within an almost perfect circular bend of the fast-flowing water, which snaked away through the mountains and lower hills, and disappeared in the distance.

"Are you thinking what I'm thinking?" asked Tilde.

"I'm thinking it's the only way," replied Mani.

Leo shook his head. "But I can't swim," he said softly.

"Don't move!" a man's voice ordered behind them. "Step away from the edge."

Mani looked back over her shoulder. Four guards had arrived on the roof, their guns raised and aimed in their direction.

Eliza appeared behind the guards. Her neat white jacket was smudged with smoke and charcoal, and her white hair was blowing wildly around her head like a snow blizzard. "They'll never jump!" she screeched over the wind. "Hold your fire! Do not harm the child!"

There was a pause. "Step away from the edge!" the guard shouted again.

Mani looked down at the moat and shuffled her feet closer to the edge. She reached out and took Leo's hand and then Tilde's.

Eliza's voice came shrieking into the hurling wind. "Take the old man," she raged, "but DO NOT harm the child!"

Mani felt Leo turn to look back at the guards. She held onto his hand—it felt cold and fragile, as if she might crush it if she held it too tightly. She turned to look at Tilde, who nodded back at her.

Mani took a step forward over the edge. As she did so, she heard the sound of a single gunshot, and her friends' hands slipped from hers. And then she was tumbling alone and fast through the air. She fell violently and noisily down, down, through the buffeting wind, until her feet hit the water with a smack. She was still falling, but through icy water now, which slashed her cheeks and body as she sank deeper. It filled her nose and mouth and ears, and bubbles of air clung to her like chains, but still she was going down, and down, until her sinking body started to slow, and finally it stopped in the dark icy depths of the water.

And then everything was quiet.

Chapter 45

Mani opened her eyes. The world was white. Endless, uninterrupted white. There was no horizon. No end to anything. Everything was perfectly still. She took a deep breath and blinked. She knew this place. But she wasn't wearing the mask. How had she got here?

Suddenly, she was falling again, but not through water; she was tumbling through clear, ice-cold air. She surrendered to the feeling, turning onto her tummy and reaching her arms and legs out either side, like a star. She waited for the impact with the ground. She wasn't scared. She knew what she would find.

But the snowy ground never came.

Something scooped her up before she landed—like a giant hand, or strong arms—and now she was being cradled in a bed of soft feathers. She could see huge, golden-brown wings either side. She lay on her tummy and felt the wind in her hair as the huge bird powered upwards. She squeezed her eyes shut and let her head rest on the feathery bed. She could hear the slow, thunderous sweep of wings beating up, down, up, down.

And she knew.

She knew who had stopped her falling.

Higher and higher Eagle carried her, and the air got thinner and colder. Finally, there was a loud whooshing sound all around her—of rushing air and folding feathers—and a sensation of braking and slowing—and then she was sliding down, trying to grasp the sleek feathers to stop herself, but she couldn't hold on. She slipped and slid until she landed with a thud on soft, snow-covered ground.

Mani opened her eyes. She was high up. On top of a mountain—maybe. She could see the horizon in the distance, and behind it a rainbow. Except it wasn't an arched rainbow—more a curtain of dancing lights—turquoise and green and orange and pink and blue and purple—all flickering and shimmering behind the horizon.

Eagle gazed down at her. The rainbow was all around now, and bright colours fell on the bird's tawny feathers. As the lights moved, and the colours changed, Eagle's face changed.

Mani gasped. They were her eyes. And it was her nose. And her smile.

Matka.

Her *matka*.

She scrambled forward and threw herself into Eagle's downy chest. She closed her eyes and buried her face. It was the warmth of her mother's embrace and the scent she knew so well. At last, she had her. She didn't want this moment to end. *Ever.* In the back of her mind—somewhere—she knew that something bad had just happened—something very bad—but right now she knew that, whatever happened next, everything would be OK.

Everything would be OK.

Mani had found her. And she would never let her go. *Ever.*

Except…

Except she had to.

Mani felt the ice and snow crumbling away beneath her feet, and the air turned to water, churning and bubbling around her head and filling her ears and nose, making her lungs burn inside her chest.

Her face broke the surface of the water and she drew in a sharp lungful of air. She felt heavy, but arms were holding her, and a hand gently angled her chin out of the water. She was on her back, being pulled along, and then she was dragged up a muddy river beach.

Tilde's face peered over her. She was frowning and her eyes were shiny. "What took you so long? I thought you'd drowned. Wow, Mani—you can't leave me. We're in this together now. I thought you'd gone!"

Mani pulled herself up and turned to face Tilde. She shivered. Her chest hurt as she tried to calm her heaving breathing—her whole body ached. The world she had just been in flashed momentarily before her eyes—rainbow lights on pure, white snow and giant, golden-brown wings. And then it was gone—and Matka was gone—but the feeling she'd had was still there.

Everything would be OK. And the knowledge that Eagle and Wolf—the spirits of Matka and Tatka—would always be there, looking out for her, protecting her, was a comfort.

Mani let her head sink back against the ground. "Sorry for almost dying…I'll try not to do that again."

Tilde's face softened and she laughed. "Well, you made it…and you're OK…but I've no idea how. You've been under that water for ages. No one can hold their breath for that long, can they? What is it with you?"

Mani pushed herself up with her elbows and looked out across the water. It twisted and eddied with deep undercurrents. The seething surface reflected only fractured shapes from the looming Ark above. Had they really jumped? How long had she been under the water for?

Then something caught her eye. From high in the air, it flitted left and right like a butterfly, carried to and fro on the breeze, until it finally landed on the beach in front of her. Mani reached forward. It was a piece of paper, torn and faded, and it fell into two pieces as she lifted it. Leo's map. And on one edge was a fingerprint—in blood.

"The map!" said Mani, looking at Tilde.

"He didn't jump with us?" Tilde looked up at the Ark.

Mani shrugged. The bloody fingerprint seemed to suggest another story that she didn't want to think about. "I don't know. Maybe…he can't swim." She looked down at the churning water and then up at the Ark. "Thanks, Leo," she said quietly.

She lay the two pieces of map on a large, dry stone, then looked up at Tilde.

"Do you remember Teodor—the man I helped— who gave us the firefly? The place he talked about? We should go there." She scrutinized the map closely. What had he said? She could see the almost circular bend in the river where the Ark was situated. She looked up. The river snaked away to the horizon, where the sun was lowering.

Tilde crouched down beside her, searching the map. "I remember! He said find the Old Man of the Taiga. What is it? Where do you think it is?"

"I'm not sure," said Mani. "Do you think it's a person? Or a thing—like the Three Sisters are mountains?" She ran her finger along the curving blue line of river. "Look—here's the horseshoe bend where the Ark is, and the river goes west, like he said." She nodded towards the sinking sun and folded the map, standing up shakily. "So, I guess there's only one way to find out!" She held her arm out to Tilde.

Tilde grinned and stood up. "Old Man of the Taiga—whoever you are—here we come!" She hooked her arm into Mani's, and together they turned to face west, taking their first steps towards the setting sun.

Chapter 46

Mani and Tilde walked and walked, following the river west. For most of the way, the river was wide and calm, and there were long stretches of shingly beach that made it easy under foot. Now and then, they stopped to scoop up handfuls of mint-clear water or to pick berries from the lower branches of trees hanging over the water. When night-time came, the moon on the river was a silver silken thread that seemed to pull them onwards. And, even though they were tired and dirty and cold, the thought of the new place that Teodor had told them about— the Taiga— and the knowledge that they were leaving the Ark far behind them, was enough to keep them going. Mani kept her eyes fixed on the horizon, searching for a sign of the Old Man.

Finally, on the third day, as the rising sun began to warm the air, in the distance, a single, tall rock set back from the river became visible. It was as tall as a tree and glowing orange, like a beacon, in the morning light. It looked like a giant standing guard and, as they got closer, the contours and lines etched onto the surface of the rock became the shadowy eyes and ragged beard of an old man. The Old Man of the Taiga! It was the sign they had been looking for and, remembering Teodor's instructions, they knew that it was time to cut away from the river and enter the forest.

They weaved their way through the trees, deeper and deeper into the forest. The sun spiked orange beams through the branches, lighting their way. Finally, they came to a long fence laced with barbed wire, and a lopsided sign. In peeling red paint, capital letters read, *PENITENTIARY: NO UNAUTHORIZED ACCESS.*

Some sections of the fence were falling down, and creeping plant life snaked in and around the barbs. On the other side, they could see there was a complex of several buildings with crumbling walls and broken windows and doors. In several places, the roofs had caved in, and the surrounding forest seemed to have taken up residence—roots and branches and leaves and vines wound their way through gaping windows and doorways, forcing the bricks and cement to give way.

They crouched side by side behind the fence and peered through the undergrowth. There were voices, and shadows were moving around inside the buildings. The nearby land had been organized and cultivated into neat gardens. Some had lines of vegetables growing, and there was a woodpile of tidily hewn logs.

"It looks like it's an old prison," said Mani. "Do you think this is it? Do you think this is the Taiga that Teodor meant?"

Tilde shrugged. "I should go in first." She looked sideways at Mani. "And find out. You hide here. We know what happens when people see you."

Mani peered through the fence. She nodded slowly. It was true. Her eyes were too noticeable. People would be scared—they would assume she had the disease and was a danger to them before she had a chance to explain and ask if Teodor was there.

"I'll wait here," she said, pointing at a huge tree with giant exposed roots that looped in and out of the ground. "It'll be easy for you to find, but I can hide too."

Tilde nodded and clambered over the broken fence. She paused and looked back at Mani. "I'll be back!" she grinned.

Mani watched her disappear into the decaying building complex. She sat down and nestled into the giant tree, curling into its embrace.

Waiting.

Again.

Hungry and thirsty.

And alone.

But, this time, inside, she had a feeling—something she knew with full certainty. It was all going to be OK.

She felt for the handle of her knife in its holster—the only one of her possessions she had managed to keep.

She pulled it out and reached up to cut a thin, green branch. She trimmed off the end and held it to her lips. The clean sap was sweet and soothing in her dry mouth.

She closed her eyes. A feeling of sadness washed through her. Leo was no longer with them. Had he jumped—or did he decide to stay? And she thought about the mask. It was lost—probably for ever—in the Ark.

There was a loud rustling in the branches above and a *"Crrrawk!"* ripped through the air. A shadow passed over her as a bird took off. And then a thought came to her. *A new mask. Could she make one?* She had her knife. She could use wood from the forest around her. And she had time—how long Tilde would be, she didn't know. Perhaps, if she made another mask, it would work in the same way?

So now, with her knife, Mani cleaved a section of wood that was already loose away from the main trunk of the giant tree. She held it in her hands and examined it. It was thin and had a natural curve that would probably mould easily to her head. It might do. There were a couple of green shoots and new leaves on one edge, which almost looked like the feather decorations on the old mask. Some of the bark was already peeling away to reveal a smooth surface, so she started to whittle more shape around the bottom edge and trim some of the bark away. She carved eye holes, and she pressed two smaller holes in each side. She searched the forest floor and found a twisting vine, which she threaded through to serve as a strap.

When she was finished, she held up her creation. She liked it. It was rougher and wonkier than the original, but it felt like part of the forest and had its own character. She ran her fingers through the leaves and stroked the smooth wooden surface and the sections of bark she had left on. She gave it her full attention and, as her focus settled, there was a shimmering of light.

Was it working? Already?

But the lights were different. Before, they had been turquoise and green, and came from the mask, but these were orange and seemed to be gathering around her head and in the lower branches of the tree. Then they dispersed and floated up above her.

There was a sudden noise in the undergrowth and the sound of crashing footsteps and excited voices. The cluster of bright lights hovered over her, illuminating the tree and the mask. They weren't coming from the mask at all. They were fireflies—fiercely bright, like the one Teodor had given her.

She heard Tilde's voice. "Here she is! She's here!"

A man's voice came next. "I can't believe it's you!"

And then there were other figures standing around her. Mani lowered the mask into her lap and looked up. It was him—Teodor, the man she had saved—crouching in front of her, his face illuminated by the orange glow from the fireflies. Tilde had found him! He was dressed in the same black hoodie—his hair was shorter, but his dark-green eyes shone their gratefulness still.

Two older women appeared at his side, both dressed in army combats.

Teodor looked up. "This is her! The girl I told you about! She cured me!"

One of the women stepped forward. She had short black curly hair and a serious expression. She stared at Mani. "Remarkable," she breathed.

Mani could tell that, although the woman was looking at her, she wasn't really seeing her. She was lost in the electricity of her eyes, and what it might mean.

The other woman had long grey hair tied back in a ponytail. Her wrinkled face opened out in the kindest smile Mani had ever seen. "Welcome to the Taiga!" she said softly. "You are very welcome here."

The curly-haired woman shook her head, as if remembering herself. "Of course…How rude of me. Please—come with us." She opened her arms and then gestured back towards the buildings. "You must be hungry. Come, eat with us—we have fresh flatbreads and tea. You are safe here."

Mani glanced at Tilde, who was grinning ear to ear. Bubbles of laughter and relief formed at the back of her throat and tears poked at her eyes.

They'd made it.

They were here.

They were safe.

Mani put the whalebone-handled knife back in its holster and tucked the new mask under her arm. As she did so, she thought she saw a faint glow of pulsing turquoise and green light.

But, for now, that could wait.

Epilogue

In which Crow tries to explain...

"Once upon a time...Twice upon a—"

"Twice a what?" Mani stumbled across the snowy land, trying to keep up with Crow, who was half galloping, half flying in front of her.

"Shush, kiddo—Q & A at the end!" Crow leaped forward with a *Crawk!* and a flourish of his jet-black wings.

"But...I just..." Mani panted.

"I know you just...," winked Crow. "I *just*, too...I *just* gotta tell you some stuff. You *just* gotta listen."

Crow stopped and shook his wings, eyeing Mani with one black, oily eye. "You got lesson one, didn't you?

Once upon a time…? You and your old bear? Now, it's time to turn the page. Lesson two."

Therc was a heavy thudding behind her. "Ooshaka!" Mani breathed. She fell into the polar bear and buried her face in the dense white fur until she couldn't tell where she ended and Ooshaka began. The *ba-ba-boom-boom* of the bear's heart beat in time with her own.

"So, kiddo…we need to rewind," Crow carried on, hopping forward. "Start again. This time, get the wide view. The big picture. Technicolour. See across this world—and into yours. You know all about the snow—what your ma and pa taught you—the time before it melted. They told you the stories. And you found it here. Because that's what we got, here—all the memories and all the stories. That's what we're made of. But what's gone wrong in your world? Why are things so broken there? And what have *you* and that mask got to do with it all?"

This was a question Mani had asked herself—why her and why a mask? What did it all mean?

"How do you like ball games, kiddo?" Crow lowered his head and tapped with his beak against a large glass ball. It rolled towards Mani and stopped in front of her. "Go on! Pick it up! Take a peek!"

Mani picked the glassy sphere up. It was the size of a football. Inside, she could see a snowy landscape beneath an ink-black night sky. As she peered in, she noticed something moving. She looked closer. There was a creature walking across the snowy land. Its fur was white and it had pointed ears and a long, full, bushy tail, raised high like a candle in the darkness. A snow fox. She tensed her hands and arms to keep the sphere still, as if moving it might disturb the creature.

A million sparks were flying all around the fox. They were spraying high up into the blue-black air inside the sphere, where they formed a beautiful starry night sky.

Mani sat down on the ground and crossed her legs. She held the sphere carefully in her lap and watched intently. The snow fox was turning circles on the snowy ground, and the sparks and stars seemed now to be gathering and whirling in shimmering blues and greens, until a spinning, dancing cloud of lights had formed inside the sphere.

"The aurora?" whispered Mani. "The Northern Lights?" She used to watch them with Matka and Tatka. They would sit together beneath the shimmering blue-green veils of light, and her mother would tell stories of their family and their ancestors. One of Mani's favourite stories was about the day of her birth—when the aurora had danced above her cradle and blessed her with their lights. At least, that's how Matka had told it. She was special—to have been born on that day, in that place, under the dancing lights of the north. She had been touched by the lights—*a gift*—and she was never to forget that.

Mani peered inside the sphere and watched the snow fox. It was settling now, and had curled up on the ground, snuggling its nose under its tail. A perfect circle. It breathed softly beneath the light show. Where its fluffy white tail touched its black nose, there was the softest downy bed—and, lying on it, sleeping peacefully, was a child. A baby.

"Like the light show then, kiddo?" whispered Crow. "Beginning to see? Like I say, once upon a time… there was a kid who was born in the north. The most northern part of the world—your world. But…," Crow held Mani's gaze now in his shiny eyes. "Twice upon a time…this kid was special. She was the right kid, born in a special place, and at a special time."

Mani tilted the sphere slightly so she could see the baby tucked inside the fox-tail nest more clearly. The lights danced all over the sleeping child. She could see a polar bear sitting close to the fox, watching over the baby. Its white fur was also illuminated by the green-blue lights. Suddenly, she understood.

"The baby…under the lights…The aurora…Is it me?"

Crow leaped up with a *crawk*. "Bingo! You got it! This kid's a genius! Special doesn't even come near it!"

So Matka's story had been true—she had been born under the aurora, and it made her special. But what did that mean?

Crow shook his feathers. "Now, I got words to say." His voice was serious and he projected it as if he was giving an important speech that he'd carefully prepared. "Are you sitting comfortably?" He didn't wait for an answer. "Then I'll begin…," he started, solemnly. "We'd all been waiting for her—the whole of this world had— to keep the connection. Between this world and yours."

Crow hopped from one foot to the other.

"Like it or not, kiddo—you are the one. The one that we all need. You were born to tread the two paths. We need you. To keep the balance. Mind and body, yin and yang, light and shade, heaven and earth—call it what you want. Our world and yours—we're losing the balance and the connection. Your world is broken—and soon ours will be. We need you to fix it."

Ooshaka spoke now for the first time. "Is it OK? Mani?" she asked gently. "Are you beginning to see? You were too young. Your mother had more to tell you. She knew. But she left you too soon."

"Keep watching, kiddo. This is where I come in," whispered Crow.

Mani looked down into the sphere again. The dark shadow of a crow flew in. But the scene had changed. The baby was no longer sleeping in the downy fur of the snow fox. And it was no longer a snow scene. It was Mani's bedroom at home, and there she was, a baby in her first cot, a dreambell hanging at one end. They were both there—Matka and Tatka—their arms around each other, smiling over their sleeping child. Crow landed on the bar of the cot. He had something in his beak, which he dropped beside baby Mani's sleeping head. Then he flew away.

Mani watched her mother pick it up and turn it over. It glowed with turquoise lights that illuminated her solemn face. Mani could see what it was, now. The mask. Matka turned around, searching for where Crow had gone. She held the mask for a moment and looked down at sleeping Mani. Then she reached up and hung it high on a hook on the wall, out of reach.

Crow whispered in her ear, "The mask—I brought it. You need it—to move between worlds. To do what you gotta do. But *it's* not special. *You* give it the power. You lost that mask—but you know that doesn't matter. Now, you've made your own and you've given it the power. You're getting the hang of it, kiddo…and now you've got work to do."

Mani looked at Crow. All of a sudden, she understood—this part, at least. She needed the mask to enter the other world—the mask world. But it was *her* that gave the mask power. *She* had the gift—to move between this world and that. The gift had been given to her when she was born. She set the ball down, now. It was beginning to make sense.

Crow flew up into the air and landed on Ooshaka's head. "You've had an adventure getting here," he crawked down to Mani, "but, I'm telling you, your biggest adventure is yet to come."

As Crow's words echoed in the air around her, somewhere in the distance Mani could hear Wolf howl, and up above her she could see Eagle turning protective circles in the never-ending blue sky. She turned and leaned into Ooshaka—letting her head rest in the bear's soft white fur.

She looked up at Crow and nodded solemnly. There was more to learn, more to do—a bigger adventure. But, right now, in the strangest of ways, she was home.

About the Author

Antonia Maxwell is a writer and freelance book editor. With a degree in modern languages, and thirty years in book publishing, she is a self-professed word nerd. As well as working with book publishers to hunt down rogue apostrophes and missing full stops, she also teaches editing skills and creative writing. In her own writing, she seeks to engage with our changing world, and foster in young readers tools of self-understanding, resilience and hope. She is based near Cambridge, where she enjoys wild swimming and walking under the big eastern skies. *Terra Electrica: The Guardians of the North* is her debut novel for children.

*Acknowledgements

I would like to thank the following people who have all helped make *Terra Electrica*.

Neem Tree Press—I am very fortunate that Mani and Ooshaka found a home with such a brilliant and outward-looking publisher. Thanks to Archna Sharma for taking it on—and for the insightful 'big picture' edits and vision for the book; Cecilia Bennett for the beautiful illustrations and masterful editorial work; Penelope Price for forensic copy-editing and final polish; Amy Jade Choi for leading the launch into the world; Alison Savage for vital nuts and bolts; Jet Purdie for the wonderful cover.

Molly's Coffee Shop Writers in Saffron Walden, Essex—thanks to Carol, Christa, Alan, Stan, Alison, Penelope, Matt, Dave, Eileen, Celia and Adrian for joyful Monday mornings in the freezing cold (probably haunted!) room at Molly's, drinking coffee, sharing writing and dissecting stories—these were the best of times.

SCWBI Central East PB/MG/YA crit group—it's been good to be in a room with fellow children's writers. Thanks in particular to Ian Wilson, Sian Mole and Sally Hewitt for their full reads of the *Terra Electrica* manuscript and their helpful and encouraging comments.

The Leckeys—thanks for being patient and encouraging sounding boards. Thanks to Maia for the cheerleading and words of wisdom (and help understanding the 'socials'); Finn for insights into worldbuilding and storytelling (especially in games and films); Theo for providing the view from science (and putting me right). Thanks to Calvin (FC) for consultancy services on all things electric (Leckey by name…)—and everything else!

Clan Maxwell (Nottingham branch)—*reviresco*!

Jessica Radcliffe-Oliver—thanks for sharing stories of power journeys and spirit animals when we were at school—and generally being the best of best friends. Thanks also to Gillian Radcliffe for a late read of the manuscript and encouraging comments.

Terra Electrica wouldn't exist if it wasn't for John Lomas-Bullivant of Kickback Media, storyworld producer for publishing, TV and film. 'Mani' started out in 2018 as a 2,000-word entry in a competition run by *The Writers' and Artists' Yearbook* and Kickback Media. It was free to enter and the prize was the opportunity

263

to develop the submission—with a view to creating a children's story suitable for publishing and film adaptation. I thought this was the best possible prize. Although Mani and her polar bear in the melted Arctic didn't win the competition, John liked them enough to go on a journey with us. He helped develop the storyworld and kickstart the story, and then encouraged and helped me to filter ideas through rigorous logic while holding on to the emotional heart. Thank you John—and sorry about the rabbit holes.

Finally, thanks to my four-footed power friends— much-missed Conker (basset-corgi) and new-kid-on-the-block Starsky (corgi)—both have accompanied me on tramps through the ancient Essex/Cambridge countryside, and helped me to unravel sticky plot points and gain inspiration from a beautiful and ever-changing landscape.